A Candlelight Ecstasy Romance

"NO, NOT YOU . . . NEVER YOU. IT'S ME. THERE'S SOMETHING WRONG WITH ME."

Very gently he smoothed her hair back from her face. "What are you talking about. You're the most nearly perfect woman I've ever known."

"Oh, God . . ." She propped her elbows on her knees and covered her face with her hands. Her muffled voice was thick with unshed tears. "You don't understand. I'm not like other women. He told me he needed me, and I tried to be what he wanted. But I couldn't . . . I couldn't . . ."

"Are you telling me you're frigid?"

She nodded, her face still hidden in '

He touched her shoulder. She wa

"April, look at me."

"Don't touch me."

His palm closed firmly about the c shoulder. For a long moment she di Then slowly she lifted her head and m His fingers brushed the tears from her ch need to be touched, love," he said wit tenderness.

218 STORMY SURRENDER, *Jessica Massey*
219 MOMENT TO MOMENT, *Bonnie Drake*
220 A CLASSIC LOVE, *Jo Calloway*
221 A NIGHT IN THE FOREST, *Alysse Rasmussen*
222 SEDUCTIVE ILLUSION, *Joanne Bremer*
223 MORNING'S PROMISE, *Emily Elliott*
224 PASSIONATE PURSUIT, *Eleanor Woods*
225 ONLY FOR LOVE, *Tira Lacy*
226 SPECIAL DELIVERY, *Elaine Raco Chase*
227 BUSINESS BEFORE PLEASURE, *Alison Tyler*
228 LOVING BRAND, *Emma Bennett*
229 THE PERFECT TOUCH, *Tate McKenna*
230 HEAVEN'S EMBRACE, *Sheila Paulos*
231 KISS AND TELL, *Paula Hamilton*
232 WHEN OPPOSITES ATTRACT, *Candice Adams*
233 TROUBLE IN PARADISE, *Antoinette Hale*
234 A BETTER FATE, *Prudence Martin*
235 BLUE RIDGE AUTUMN, *Natalie Stone*
236 BEGUILED BY A STRANGER, *Eleanor Woods*
237 LOVE, BID ME WELCOME, *JoAnna Brandon*
238 HEARTBEATS, *Jo Calloway*
239 OUT OF CONTROL, *Lori Copeland*
240 TAKING A CHANCE, *Anna Hudson*
241 HOURS TO CHERISH, *Heather Graham*
242 PRIVATE ACCOUNT, *Cathie Linz*
243 THE BEST THINGS IN LIFE, *Linda Vail*
244 SETTLING THE SCORE, *Norma Brader*
245 TOO GOOD TO BE TRUE, *Alison Tyler*
246 SECRETS FOR SHARING, *Carol Norris*
247 WORKING IT OUT, *Julia Howard*
248 STAR ATTRACTION, *Melanie Catley*
249 FOR BETTER OR WORSE, *Linda Randall Wisdom*
250 SUMMER WINE, *Alexis Hill Jordan*
251 NO LOVE LOST, *Eleanor Woods*
252 A MATTER OF JUDGMENT, *Emily Elliott*
253 GOLDEN VOWS, *Karen Whittenburg*
254 AN EXPERT'S ADVICE, *Joanne Bremer*
255 A RISK WORTH TAKING, *Jan Stuart*
256 GAME PLAN, *Sara Jennings*
257 WITH EACH PASSING HOUR, *Emma Bennett*

PROMISE OF SPRING

Jean Hager

A CANDLELIGHT ECSTASY ROMANCE®

Published by
Dell Publishing Co., Inc.
1 Dag Hammarskjold Plaza
New York, New York 10017

Dell ® TM 681510, Dell Publishing Co., Inc.
Candlelight Ecstasy Romance®, 1,203,540, is a registered trademark
of Dell Publishing Co., Inc., New York, New York.

ISBN: 0-440-17312-4

Printed in the United States of America
First printing—August 1984

To Our Readers:

We have been delighted with your enthusiastic response to Candlelight Ecstasy Romances®, and we thank you for the interest you have shown in this exciting series.

In the upcoming months we will continue to present the distinctive, sensuous love stories you have come to expect only from Ecstasy. We look forward to bringing you many more books from your favorite authors and also the very finest work from new authors of contemporary romantic fiction.

As always, we are striving to present the unique, absorbing love stories that you enjoy most—books that are more than ordinary romance.

Your suggestions and comments are always welcome. Please write to us at the address below.

Sincerely,

The Editors
Candlelight Romances
1 Dag Hammarskjold Plaza
New York, N.Y. 10017

CHAPTER ONE

April dashed through the door to the Forum. Workmen were resurfacing the ice-skating rink on the ground floor and a few early shoppers were already wandering about as she took the escalator to the third level.

She paused to admire the boutique's window display which she and Val Winston, her only full-time employee, had arranged the evening before. On one side of the window, red and green party gowns in satin and crepe were draped at the foot of a snow-flecked tree. The subdued artificial lighting heightened the material's soft folds. On the other side, elves worked on silver slippers and glittering gold and silver necklaces. One red-haired elf, who reminded April of Rusty, was arranging a silver fox stole in a gift box.

As she thought of her six-year-old son a smile softened her expression. Rusty was hers alone now; no one could ever take him away from her. After a year she still experienced a flood of relief every time she reminded herself of that. Freedom. It was wonderful! She would not let the irrational fears that had plagued her for months after Paul's death come back to haunt her now. That part of her life was over.

She swallowed the tightness that rose in her throat and returned her attention to the window, looking at it from several angles. She and Val had changed the Christmas display every week since Thanksgiving, but this one was the most attractive yet, which was fitting, April thought, since Christmas was now only six days away.

She let herself into the shop. It was nine thirty and April's didn't open until ten. She shed her coat, turned on the lights, and glanced over the boutique to satisfy herself that everything was in place, ready for the busy day ahead. As always, she was pleased with what she saw —walls and thick velvety carpeting of creamy ivory, counters in antique white and gold, delicately carved gold latticed screens separating the various areas, tasteful displays of clothing and jewelry.

The boutique carried some expensive lines and April had wanted understated elegance as a background for the merchandise. Her best friend, Elana Pritchett, had designed the interior, translating into colors and textures April's sometimes fuzzy mental pictures. The boutique was not just a perfect setting for fashionable merchandise. It was also a display area of sorts for April herself, with her tall, slender figure, smooth ivory complexion, black hair, and large brown eyes.

The bell on the shop door jingled and, startled, April turned toward the sound. A tall man wearing a tweed topcoat had entered the boutique; she had forgotten to lock the door behind her.

"Looks as though I'm your first customer." His voice was deep and appealingly rough.

"Yes." Now that he was inside, she couldn't tell him the boutique didn't open until ten. A quick survey convinced her that his suit and coat bore a top designer's label. She couldn't afford to turn away an obviously affluent customer even had she been so inclined. "May I help you?"

He shrugged out of the topcoat and folded it over his

arm. His six feet plus of leanness wore the finely tailored navy suit well. The snowy triangle above his vest was dissected by a navy and white striped tie. His shirt was a stark whiteness in contrast with the deeply tanned skin of his face and throat. He had evidently spent some time in a tropical climate recently. Dark brown hair was brushed into a smooth style, shaped neatly to his head. Thick eyebrows that almost met over his nose gave him a rakish look. Deep blue eyes gazed at her from beneath heavy lashes. Hard planes of jaw, nose, and cheekbone prevented handsomeness. Her customer was utterly male; this and his size made him seem ludicrously out of place against the pale, feminine background of the boutique.

"I'll look around," he said, strolling over to a rack of designer nightgowns. He shoved the hangers back on the rod, one by one, with his big hand. He took a blue silk gown off the rack and held it up to examine it, his head cocked to one side. "What size is this one?"

April walked to his side and glanced at the tag dangling from the sleeve of the gown. "Thirty-four," she said.

His blue eyes narrowed as he turned his attention from the gown to her. "That's the breast size?"

April winced inwardly. "The bust size, yes."

He smiled at that and April felt a warmth invading her cheeks. What an absurd reaction, she chided herself. It wasn't so rare an occurrence, helping a husband or boyfriend choose something for the woman in his life. Which was he, she wondered, husband or boyfriend? She was surprised at the strength of her impulse to glance at his left hand to see if he wore a wedding ring. But she fought it off.

He considered her for a moment, giving her his full

11

attention for the first time since he'd entered the boutique. The blue eyes glittered with intelligence and awareness of her as a woman.

"I'm not sure what size I want," he drawled as he slowly perused her finely structured face, the arching black brows, thick dark lashes, generous lips and high cheekbones that hinted at Indian ancestry somewhere down the line. Her black hair was pulled back into a smooth chignon. Faint smudges of shadow beneath the liquid brown eyes made him wonder if she was unhappy. Such a beautiful woman shouldn't be unhappy. Maybe she disliked working in the boutique. His gaze wandered lower over the sleek lines of her black wool dress. "What size are you?"

It was a perfectly legitimate question, but April's stomach reacted as if he'd whispered an erotic suggestion into her ear. She swallowed. "This would fit me," she replied coolly.

"Ah . . ." He returned the blue gown to the rod. "It'll have to be bigger then. Maybe a forty."

April had managed to get a glimpse of his left hand; it was ringless. So he must want the gown for his girlfriend, who was evidently very generously endowed. Not that April was surprised. He struck her as a man who would want his companion to be all woman. And maybe he was one of those macho characters who correlated femininity with a big bust measurement. For some reason April found the thought disappointing.

"This is the only forty we have at the moment." She pulled out a white gown with a modestly scooped neckline and long sleeves gathered at the wrist. She didn't think he would like it; it covered too much.

To her surprise he appeared to give the gown serious

consideration. Finally he shook his head. "It doesn't look like her."

"Perhaps you could tell me something about her," April said, "and I might be able to suggest something."

His features rearranged themselves into a fond smile. "Rosie's got red hair and green eyes. She's down-to-earth and the best cook in Oklahoma."

A red-headed, earthy little homebody, April thought, disliking the woman immediately. She probably has the brain of a turnip and a body like Raquel Welch's. The thought caught her up short. What was wrong with her? She'd never even seen the woman. Rosie was undoubtedly a perfectly nice person. "Perhaps something a little more prosaic then," she suggested, turning away from the expensive designer gowns. "These velveteen robes have been very popular with our customers." She took a dark blue robe from one of the circular racks in the center of the showroom. "As you can see, the cut is—er, generous. And this color is attractive with red hair."

One of his dark eyebrows arched above a twinkling blue eye. The last reaction April had been trying to evoke was this sudden male amusement. It vexed her. She'd better get her uncharacteristic flights of fancy under control if she wanted to make this sale, she cautioned herself.

"Will you gift-wrap it?"

"Of course." She carried the robe to the cash register counter and bent to pull a box from the shelf beneath. She put the box together, bending and tucking in the corners. Folding the robe, she swathed it in tissue paper before closing the lid.

He had followed her to the counter and was lounging against it, his arms folded, watching her. "Have you worked here long?"

13

"About ten months." She cut a length of gold foil paper from a roll and wrapped it around the box, securing the edges with transparent tape.

"Do you like it?"

"Very much."

He was silent for an instant, watching her. "Do you have plans for lunch?"

She glanced up sharply. The deep blue eyes glittered with promise. Was this stranger asking her for a date? Why that should make her feel so nervous, she didn't know. Perhaps because she hadn't had a date in a very long time. And did Rosie know her boyfriend had a roving eye?

She dropped her eyes and pulled about a yard of wide silver ribbon from its roll. She fashioned a large bow with quick, deft movements. "We'll probably send out for something. We'll be very busy later on." She named the price and he wrote out a check. The signature was "Victor Leyland." April tucked it beneath the cash drawer and turned back to him. She said with a dismissing smile, "If Rosie prefers something else, she can exchange the robe."

"Oh, she won't want to exchange it," he stated with assurance. "She'll be crazy about it. Rosie's the easiest woman to please I ever knew."

Good old Rosie, April thought, her smile slipping. "Well, thank you for shopping at April's."

She placed the gift-wrapped package on top of the counter, but he ignored it. "What about dinner?"

"Are you asking me for a date, Mr. Leyland?" she inquired with evident disbelief.

He grinned wickedly. "I thought I was being clear enough." He bowed slightly in mock politeness. "Will

14

you do me the honor of having dinner with me this evening, Miss . . ."

She stared at him with baleful skepticism. "No, thank you, Mr. Leyland."

"Why not?" he persisted, undaunted.

"I should think," she retorted, "that would be obvious."

"Oh, hell," he muttered, "you're married."

"No . . . it isn't that."

He bent over the counter until his face was very close to hers. "Is that a blush, Miss . . . What *is* your name?"

She backed up a step. His nearness discomfited her. "Dubois," she said curtly. "And, no, I'm not blushing. I'm simply amazed. You don't know me from Adam."

"As good a reason as any for having dinner. We'll get acquainted."

"It's out of the question."

"Hmmm." He looked at her interestedly. "I think I understand. Your boss doesn't allow you to fraternize with the customers."

She blinked and seized the excuse. "Er—exactly."

He smiled slowly. "Your boss doesn't own you, Miss Dubois."

She released a sigh. "Mr. Leyland, I can't believe you're so hard up you have to ask chance-met strangers to have dinner with you."

"Only the pretty ones," he retorted, not at all stung.

She shook her head a little dazedly. "Does Rosie know you do this kind of thing?"

He looked startled for an instant, and then he threw back his head and laughed. Finally he said, "Rosie knows me inside out, and she loves me anyway."

"More fool she," April murmured.

15

He slanted a dark look down at her as he picked up his package. "I have to get to work now, Miss Dubois. Perhaps we'll continue this conversation another time."

Something flickered awake in April at the mocking invitation in his drawling voice. Something instinctive and feminine. Something so long buried that she had imagined it beyond reviving.

"I don't think so, Mr. Leyland." She reproved him with a finality she didn't altogether feel.

"I feel it's only fair to warn you Miss Dubois, that I can never resist a challenge," he retorted, a grin playing about his wide mouth.

He walked out of the shop before she could think of a suitable rejoinder. She shook her head to clear it of the bemusement left in Victor Leyland's wake. Glancing at her watch, she saw that it was fifteen minutes before ten. Victor Leyland had been in the shop exactly fifteen minutes. It seemed much longer. Suddenly a soft chuckle escaped her. He was probably an incurable flirt whose bark was far worse than his bite. Chances were she'd never see him again.

She locked the door and went to her office at the back of the shop. She started coffee in the electric percolator, and gave herself a brief businesslike inspection in the bathroom mirror.

Only those persistent shadows beneath her liquid brown eyes suggested that she had not fully recovered from years of deep unhappiness.

She could not be sure at what moment during the past few days she had become aware of the constricted feeling in her chest again. Fortunately, the pain wasn't as intense as it had been a year ago. She suspected the sensation had been triggered by the sights and sounds of the holiday

16

season. They had brought back with such force the closing days of the previous year, when everything had been suffused with the final, irrevocable knowledge that she would never be able to leave Paul without losing Rusty.

She had tried to put a brave face on things for Rusty's sake, but after the judge had handed down his decision and she had been forced to go back to Paul, just getting up in the morning had required monumental effort. Somehow, in spite of her depression, she had made herself put up a tree and shop for Rusty's gifts. Christmas Day had been a nightmare. Paul's parents, Noble and Anna Dubois, had come for the day, and the strain between them and April had been palpable.

Finally Anna cornered her in the kitchen before dinner. "April, I don't know what your problems were before you and Paul reconciled. I don't want to know. But, dear, every marriage has its rough spots. Just give it time and everything will turn out for the best."

April did not look up from the salad she was making. Anna's simplistic viewpoint no longer surprised her. "Don't worry about us, Anna. We'll be all right." She liked her mother-in-law, but the woman could not possibly understand what April had been through, even if she told her. April would not have been able to do that in any case. If Anna ever learned the truth about Paul, it would destroy her. Anna and Noble doted on their only son and neither of them, April was sure, would believe him capable of the cold, calculating cruelty April had lived with for years.

Noble Dubois was one of the wealthiest men in the southwest, a self-made millionaire. He'd come to Tulsa in the mid-fifties with nothing but his wife, small son, and a battered old Ford. Having had some experience as a construction worker, he'd borrowed money to build a house, which he'd sold when it was completed at a nice profit. That was the beginning of the Dubois Company. Noble went on to build 12,000 multi-family residential units in sixteen states. Now he traveled in a Rolls Royce Silver Spur or his private jet. April was sure that Noble himself didn't know how much he was worth. To do him credit, he had been generous with gifts of money and time to the city that had given him a chance. At one time or other he'd sat on every corporate, bank, and hospital board of any consequence in the state. His influence was prodigious. As his son, Paul, grew up, he was given everything his heart desired and some things he hadn't even thought of yet, from hand-tailored suits to forty-thousand-dollar sports cars.

For years Noble had been grooming Paul to take over control of the business when Noble retired. In fact, Paul had made something of a name for himself as a public speaker. With his thick, red hair and ready, boy-next-door grin, Paul looked very much like his father and had adopted Noble's style of speaking. He was such a good actor that even his own parents did not seem to suspect he was a consummate hypocrite. Paul had fooled them and the people he worked with just as he had fooled April until after they were married.

When April had continued chopping vegetables for the salad, saying nothing more for several moments, Anna went on. "Think of Rusty, dear. That little boy needs both his parents—together and happy."

April's patience slipped for a moment. "You don't achieve happiness merely by deciding to. I only wish it were that easy. Sometimes you have to live with one kind of unhappiness to avoid a worse kind."

"You sound so cynical. Surely things aren't so terrible. Look around you, April. You have a fine husband and son, this beautiful home, everything—"

"Anna," April interrupted, "I'm not up to counting my blessings just now. But I do think of Rusty—constantly. Oh, I know Paul's lawyer made it sound in court as if I weren't considering my son when I filed for his custody. But, believe me, he's the only reason I'm back in this house."

Anna's plain, kind face crumpled. "I hope you aren't blaming Noble for Judge Rankin's decision in the custody trial. They're old friends, but Noble didn't do anything to influence the outcome. Truly, he didn't."

Regretting her small outburst, April managed a wan smile. "I know he didn't." She didn't bother to add the obvious, that Noble Dubois didn't have to do anything. He merely had to be who he was, one of the wealthiest and most powerful men in the state, to insure that his son, the heir apparent to his empire, would win any battle for the custody of Noble Dubois's grandson. What judge or jury would decide that taking Rusty out of an obviously secure, affluent environment would be in his best interest?

Paul hadn't even had to prove that April was unfit. He merely had to smile charmingly and answer the judge's questions in the calm, confiding tone he had cultivated for his public appearances to convince everyone that he was a wonderful husband and father whose wife must be slightly demented not to appreciate her good fortune. When it was brought out in court that April was under the care of a physician for "a nervous condition," everyone's suspicions seemed to be confirmed: she was unstable, had probably made Paul's life miserable, and he was to be admired for trying to keep his family together.

Finally Anna sighed and said, "This modern, permissive society! Honestly, I don't know what young women want these days. In my day, a husband who provided for them and a comfortable home were enough."

April couldn't help chuckling. It was the first time she had felt like laughing in weeks. "Anna, you and I will never see eye to eye, that's for sure."

Anna gave her a perplexed look, and April's amusement evaporated as quickly as it had come. Her mother-in-law had some admirable qualities, but the ability to laugh at herself wasn't one of them.

Noble Dubois wasn't as naive as his wife. Before he and Anna left he took April aside. "You're an intelligent woman, my dear. Your life may not be exactly as you would like it to be, but you're sensible enough to try to make the best of it. I admire that."

"Where were you when I needed a character witness in court?" April responded with a dry edge to the words.

Noble's laugh sounded forced. "I see you still have a sense of humor too. You won't be sorry you came back to Paul, April. I'm having a trust fund set up in your name, in addition to the one I've already established for Rusty."

April, whose nerves were frayed from the strain she had been under since returning to Paul, spoke sharply. "I don't want your money, Noble. As for the other, I *am* sorry I have to stay married to Paul in order to keep my son. I will always be sorry about that, and I won't be hypocrite enough to pretend otherwise. We've enough hypocrisy in this family as it is."

He looked faintly troubled. "I know my son has his

20

faults, but who doesn't? He loves you, April. You must know that a divorce would destroy him."

April made a bitter sound. "You will forgive me, Noble, if I'm not overly concerned about Paul's feelings. I have all I can say grace over trying to salvage something of my own life. And don't talk to me about his faults as if they are nothing but naughty little habits. You can't even imagine how many or how great they are."

Fortunately Anna interrupted them then, or April might have been tempted to enlighten Noble concerning a few of his son's more glaring "little habits"—the clandestine affairs with other women, the physical and psychological abuse he practiced on his wife, the total lack of human compassion that made his family-man image a travesty.

After her in-laws had gone, April put Rusty to bed, then went into the bathroom to shower and get ready to retire herself. She couldn't remember when she had felt so weary and could hardly keep her eyes open until she had stepped from the tub, dried herself, and slipped into a nightgown. She thought she would even be able to get to sleep without tossing for hours for a change. It had been a grueling day.

Upon returning to the adjoining bedroom, she learned that worse was to come. Paul, still in the gray cashmere sweater and wool flannel trousers he had worn all day, lounged on the bed.

He let his hazel eyes run over her insolently before he asked, "What did you say to my father in the hallway just before they left?"

April hesitated to get into her bed while he was stretched out on the other side of it. Instead, she went quickly to the closet and put on a robe. "I can't remember. I was probably thanking him again for all the presents. Why?"

"He told me he hoped I had forgiven you for filing for the divorce and custody of Rusty. He advised me to do my Christian duty and let bygones be bygones."

She didn't trust Paul in this relaxed, chatty pose. "Well, it wasn't anything I said. He probably sensed things aren't good between us. You don't have to be particularly perceptive to see that."

He came up off the bed in one swift movement. "Liar." His voice was low, menacing. He walked slowly toward her. She started to back away, but he grabbed her arm and jerked her against him. "What did you tell him?"

She hated the trembling that took hold of her, exposing her fear to him. "He—he said that he admired me, that I was sensible. I asked why he hadn't mentioned that in court."

He stared down at her, his eyes glittering with the inordinate rage that he managed to keep hidden from everyone but her. He was a man filled with contempt and hatred for other people. She had never understood why, what had twisted and deformed his soul. She no longer even tried to understand; she merely tried to shield herself and Rusty from that rage as much as possible.

"What else did you say?"

He was twisting her arm painfully, and her knees almost buckled. "Nothing!"

He shoved her away so that her legs struck the bed, and she fell back across it. She lay there, staring up at him, knowing that it was wiser not to struggle. But it took all of her will not to try to bolt from the room.

"What did you and Mother talk about when you were in the kitchen together?"

22

She tried to quiet the heaving of her chest. "Nothing important. We—we talked about Rusty."

"What about him?"

She made an effort to pull her robe together over her legs. "I can't recall every word we said, Paul! For heaven's sake, leave me alone! I'm tired and I want to go to bed."

He leaned over her, stared at her for a long, taut moment, then spat out, "You make me sick, April. You don't have to use that old 'too tired' excuse. I wouldn't touch you with a ten-foot pole. Go to bed! I'm going out."

He slammed out of the house. Shaken and relieved that he hadn't demanded his "husbandly rights," April crawled into bed, her mind going feverishly along familiar paths. She had to get away from him. But she could not go and leave Rusty behind. Could she take her son and run, take on a new identity somewhere far away from Tulsa? But even in her most desperate moments she knew that she could not stay hidden long. Noble Dubois had money and influence enough to find her, no matter where she went.

In the boutique's office a year later, April wondered again what she would have done if fate had not intervened. On New Year's Eve Paul left town alone. April didn't ask where he was going because she didn't care. Besides, she felt fairly certain that he was going to Oklahoma City to see the young wife of a wealthy friend of Noble's. April knew that Paul had been carrying on an affair with the woman for months. She was simply relieved that he would be out of the house for the evening. She and Rusty made popcorn and hot chocolate and played checkers until Rusty's bedtime. She tucked him in and returned to the den to watch a videotaped movie. The house was cozy and quiet, and she couldn't help thinking how wonderful it would be if it could always be like that, if Paul would go away and never come back.

Which is what happened, but in a way that she could not have imagined. Sometime between three A.M. and dawn, his sports car went off the road, hit a concrete culvert, turned over several times, and burst into flames. He was returning to Tulsa and he was alone. It was months before April could think about it without thinking that she had wished him dead. It was an indication of her bruised emotional state that she was riddled with guilt over the death of a man she had come to loathe and fear.

During the past year April's twenty-ninth birthday had come and gone almost unnoticed as she plunged with singlemindedness into making a success of her first business venture, April's, bought and set up with Paul's insurance money. She had rebuilt her life around the shop and her son, Paul Russell Dubois II. The boutique and Rusty. They had saved her life and her sanity. Now if she could only get through the holiday season, the dark days of pain and guilt would, at last, be behind her.

She tried to shrug off a persistent anxiety. If she had gotten through Paul's funeral, she could get through anything, she told herself. After the funeral the days had taken on a sameness. She had gone through the motions of caring for Rusty and the house. Sometimes a feeling of being set free surfaced, but she pushed it down with her guilt. She didn't trust this new, unexpected freedom yet. Then one cold day in mid-February, Elana had marched into her bedroom, where she was sitting alone in the darkness with the draperies drawn.

24

Was this how April intended to spend the rest of her life, Elana wanted to know. What about Rusty? Did April realize she was hurting her son by cloistering the both of them there?

April had looked up at her friend lifelessly. "I know you're trying to help, but I just can't shake the feeling that Noble is going to walk in here any day and take Rusty away."

"You're being paranoid."

"Maybe," April admitted. "But he and Anna worshiped Paul and now they have no one but Rusty."

"I know you resent Noble for not coming to your defense at the trial, but he could hardly have taken your side against his own son. But Paul's gone now. Stop borrowing trouble. Okay?"

April nodded glumly.

"What you need is a job."

April pushed the heavy weight of her black hair off her forehead and stared at Elana. "Paul's insurance and investments will provide for me and Rusty."

"That's not the point." Elana stared back at her, and for a moment April felt a stirring of anger at her friend's seeming unconcern for what she had been through with Paul and, later, the guilt over his death.

She tossed back her hair and glared at her friend. It was the first sign of the old April who, before she had married Paul, had been vibrant and energetic and involved.

"You've got to get out of this house," Elana persisted. "Go to work in an office, a shop. Or start a business. I don't care what you do, but do something. You're going to make yourself crazy staying shut up in this mausoleum."

But it's the only place where I feel safe. "I'll think about it," April said finally.

"Good," Elana snapped. "Rusty needs his mother back." A flicker of a smile crossed Elana's face then. "I'd kind of like to have my best friend back too."

Two days later, on a Saturday, April decided to take Elana's advice and get out of the house. She drove downtown to the Forum, downtown Tulsa's modern shopping mall, part of an ambitious renovation project.

The ice-skating rink on the ground level was filled with laughing youngsters while others crowded into the eating establishments that surrounded the rink. Strolling through the mall, hearing the happy sounds of the skaters, smelling the food, April had begun to feel alive again.

She had gone home to think about a vacant shop she had noticed in the mall. Eventually she had decided to open a boutique.

Six months later, with the boutique beginning to turn a nice profit, she sold the big house on the southern outskirts of the city and moved Rusty and her housekeeper, Nan Mead, into the attractive apartment complex where Elana lived. The river park was nearby, and it was just three miles from the boutique. Selling the house had forced her to dispose of Paul's things; it had helped to banish the smothering sense of his presence that continued to linger.

From her office April could see the wet, glittering street, the wide stairs leading to the Williams Plaza Hotel and, beyond that, to the main mall where she could glimpse balls of pale light; the mall lamps still glowed against the murky grayness of the day. She remembered waiting for Paul in the lobby of the Williams Plaza, where they were to have dinner. She hadn't wanted to

26

have dinner out; by that time she had been totally disillusioned with her marriage. But Paul had insisted. And then he hadn't come, and she'd gone home alone. Later she had learned he'd been with another woman.

Turning away from the window, she poured herself a cup of freshly brewed coffee. Her hand shook slightly as she lifted the cup to her lips. She had to forget Paul and the past. She owed it to Rusty. Only that morning Rusty had begged to go ice skating. On an impulse she decided that she would finish work early, leaving Val to lock up, and go and collect Rusty for a couple of hours of skating on the rink below.

That proved easier decided than done. The boutique was filled with customers all day. A surprising number of them were men, shopping for gifts for wives or sweethearts. They were attracted by the window display. And whenever a man entered the shop, the grinning blue-eyed image of Victor Leyland flashed into April's mind, and she brushed it away with chagrin. What was it about that man that wouldn't let her forget him?

Val and her part-time-student clerks were kept so busy all day that there was no time for lunch breaks. About two, April went out for hamburgers for all of them. When she returned, she abandoned her office work for the day and waited on customers herself while her employees ate in shifts.

There was a lull about four and April mentioned to Val her plan to leave early.

"You go on," Val said promptly. "You could use a break. You're looking tired lately."

Seeing Val's concern in her expression, April felt a rush of gratitude for the bustling, gray-haired woman who had decided to go back to work when her youngest child entered college.

"Are you sure?" April said. "Things could get frantic again later on. If I hadn't had so little time with Rusty lately, I wouldn't even think of it."

"Go on!" Val made a shooing motion with her hands. "You need to be with Rusty. They grow up too fast, believe me. Don't worry about a thing."

April went into her office for her coat and, as she left the boutique, she called over her shoulder, "If you need me, you know where to find me."

She hurried through a crowd of shoppers. The pleasant, mingled smells of fresh-baked pastry, popcorn, and hot dogs from the restaurants surrounding the rink floated on the air as she took the down escalator. She left the Forum, heading for the lot where her car was parked. It had been snowing since mid-afternoon. The benches and trees on the main mall were covered with a dusting of white in the gray light of early dusk. The shops that faced the mall threw amber pools on the snow from ground-floor windows. Wreaths of pine cones and holly with red ribbons were tied to the shop doors. The smell of pine hung in the air.

April lifted her face and let the feathery flakes splatter against her skin. The sky was a dense pewter against which the towering office buildings appeared as angled, black silhouettes. It was cold and she shivered. At the same time her spirits lifted as she thought of spending some time with Rusty.

Love for her son welled up in her, bringing the hot sting of tears to her eyes. She lowered her head, blinking, and watched her shoes follow the slushy path made in the snow by shoppers. She was so lucky. She had the apartment and Nan Mead to look after things there. She had a few good friends, like Elana. She had the boutique. She had Rusty. And she had control of her own life; she was free. It was enough for her.

With the persistence of a tongue probing a sore tooth, the memory of a pair of twinkling blue eyes swam in front of her again. She shook her head and lifted her chin. She didn't want another man in her life, taking charge and making demands. Her cold shell was firmly in place and there was no danger of its melting. She'd been hurt enough already to last a lifetime.

CHAPTER TWO

It was after eight when April turned off Riverside Drive and entered the parking garage of her apartment building. Beside her, Rusty rested his drooping head against her arm.

"Hey, sport, we're home."

He straightened, yawned, and looked up at her with a sleepy smile. "We had fun, didn't we? When can we go ice skating again?"

April tousled his red hair. "Let my poor ankles recover before you mention going again! I'm not in shape for another visit to the rink right away."

"You only fell down two times. You didn't do so bad."

"Gee, thanks, but my bottom doesn't agree with you."

Rusty giggled. "You looked funny when you fell, sort of surprised."

"Oh, yeah? Well, you have a weird sense of humor and no pity at all for your klutzy mother."

He got on his knees on the seat and gave her a resounding kiss on the cheek. "I love you, Mom!"

She hugged his warm little body against her fiercely for a moment. "Oh, honey, I love you too."

He squirmed in her arms. "You're squeezing too tight."

She let him go and opened the door. He clambered out through the passenger door and took her hand companionably as they crossed the lighted parking garage and entered the building. They walked along the carpeted corridor, still holding hands, and Rusty said, "I bet Nan will be happy when we tell her she doesn't have to cook our dinner." Rusty had eaten two hot dogs at the rink.

"I called her earlier to let her know we wouldn't be home for dinner. She said she'd have some fruit and milk for you before you go to bed."

"She thinks hot dogs don't have enough vitamins and stuff," Rusty confided.

"She's probably right. So remember to take your vitamin tablet."

Rusty made a face. "If I forget, Nan will remind me." He brightened then. "Did I tell you? She's going to take David and me to the park tomorrow so we can make a snowman." David was Rusty's friend, whose family lived in the same apartment complex.

"Let's see." April pretended to think about it. "Yes, I believe you've told me that five times already."

They had reached their apartment and April unlocked the door. In the foyer, she hung their coats in the closet while Rusty preceded her into the living room.

An instant later his delighted voice reached her. "Grandpa! I didn't know you were coming to see us today."

"I wasn't sure I'd have the time until the last minute. So I decided to surprise you."

April followed Rusty into the room. "Hello, Noble."

"April, how are you?"

"Very well, thank you."

Noble sat on the sapphire velvet sofa with his arms around Rusty, who stood between his legs. "We went ice skating," Rusty told his grandfather. "And we had hot dogs and chocolate milk. It was fun!"

April took the champagne-colored velvet chair that was positioned at a right angle to the sofa. "I hope you haven't been waiting long, Noble."

"Only fifteen minutes. Nan said you should be back soon. She said it would be all right if I waited."

"I wish you'd gone ice skating with us," Rusty said.

Noble laughed, that rich, melodious sound that had charmed so many people. "I've no desire to break a leg, young man."

"Mom fell down. It was funny."

"When I agreed to take him skating, I never meant to provide the ice show too," April said with a laugh. "I'd forgotten how hard it is on the ankles."

"Her bottom's sore," Rusty chortled. "But mine isn't, and I fell down more than she did."

"I expect that's only because your bottom didn't have so far to go before it hit the ice," Noble said. "I want you to tell me all about it later, Rusty, but I'd like to talk to your mother first. Okay?"

Rusty's brown eyes rested gravely on Noble's face. "Okay, if you promise to come and see me before you leave."

"I will, I promise."

"Come on, sport," April said. "It's time you had your bath, anyway. We'll go find Nan." She led the reluctant little boy into the den, where Nan Mead was knitting and watching television. "He's practically asleep on his feet, Nan," April said.

The housekeeper put her knitting aside. "Then we'd better run your bath water, Rusty. Come on."

"Can I use some of your bubble bath, Mom?"

"Okay, but don't waste it. A few drops will make lots of bubbles." She bent to hug him. " 'Night, honey."

Rusty followed Nan down the hallway and April returned to the living room. From her seat in the armchair she looked at Noble with a slight feeling of wariness. Whenever she saw Noble she was invariably conscious of the power and influence at his command. He was one of the few people she knew for whom most rules could be circumvented. It made dealing with him an uneasy state of affairs at times.

"Rusty seems healthy and happy," Noble commented. He crossed one navy-wool-trousered leg over the other, and his foot in a black loafer of Italian leather swung slightly. One hand smoothed back the thick red hair that glistened with silver.

"He is. He's adjusted well to school and has made friends with a couple of other children in the apartment complex. In fact, one of the boys in his first-grade class lives a few doors down the hall."

"I confess, I wasn't sure you were doing the right thing when you decided to sell the house and move into an apartment."

"We're much more conveniently located here," April said, trying not to sound defensive. "As long as Rusty is content, I like apartment living. I don't have to worry about repairs and keeping up the yard." She had explained to Noble her reasons for wanting to sell the house before—omitting, of course, the main purpose, which was to erase as many reminders of Paul from her life as possible. She was repeating herself because she felt uneasy about his unscheduled visit. Rusty spent time with his grandparents fairly often, but the visits were always arranged well in advance. And neither Noble nor Anna was in the habit of dropping in on the spur of the moment.

"Are you really all right, April?" Noble asked suddenly. "You look tired."

She shrugged slightly. "I am, a little. This is the busiest time of the year at the boutique. But I'll recover quickly after the holidays."

"You don't have to work. I'm more than willing to provide comfortably for you and Rusty so you can be at home with him. I've told you that before."

"Yes, and I've told you I enjoy running my own business. I have to do something with my life besides be a mother. I'm not neglecting Rusty. Except for heavy shopping seasons, I usually manage to get home before five o'clock during the week, and I spend every weekend with him. And Nan's here all the time."

"Since you're so busy with the boutique now, I hope you'll agree to a plan hatched by Anna and me. We're going up to Shangri-la for a few days after Christmas, and we'd like to take Rusty with us." Shangri-la was a luxury resort an hour and a half's drive from Tulsa. Noble owned a condominium there. It was one of the few places where he could get away from the constant demands on his time.

"How many days will you be away?" Rusty's grandparents had never taken him out of town before. The prospect made April feel apprehensive, but she realized, too, that part of her reluctance was selfishness. The apartment would be lonely without Rusty.

"Four or five days. We thought we'd go the twenty-eighth and stay until after the new year." He leaned forward on the couch and said earnestly, "It would mean a great deal to Anna. She still misses Paul so much."

April sighed. "I know. It's just that it's quite a distance and—"

35

He shook his head sadly. "You don't trust me. You haven't since Paul died. Why, April?"

She looked at the Christmas tree in the corner. Red lights winked on and off. "I don't want Rusty to be upset. I don't want his loyalties divided."

He gazed at his hands and rubbed them together. "Surely you don't think Anna and I want that either."

There was a brief silence. She heard the wind sighing and the snow splashing on the windowpanes. "No, I don't think you do—consciously. But I know how important Rusty is to you now that Paul is gone. The worst thing we could do to Rusty would be to put him through another custody trial. He was so young the other time that he didn't fully understand what was happening. Now . . ."

He looked up at her. "Have you been thinking all this time that I'd try to take Rusty away from you?"

She met his gaze for a moment before she responded. "It must have crossed your mind. I suspect that Anna has probably mentioned it to you."

He looked away again, flushing slightly, and she knew that she had come too close to the truth. "Anna lives a confined, protected existence. She rarely sees all the ramifications of a situation." He swung his gaze back to April's troubled face. "But you needn't worry about Anna. I make the decisions in the family." April was well aware of this and the fact that Anna honestly felt her husband knew best about everything. It was the kind of blind, subservient devotion that April had never been able to give to Paul. Part of the trouble in her marriage had stemmed from the fact that Paul had expected her to be like his mother.

"If we ever should have to go to court over Rusty,"

April said quietly, "Anna would be hurt as much as anyone. I wouldn't hold anything back, Noble."

His ruddy face went very still. The tree lights continued their unceasing blinking. He stared at them as if he might find an answer there. Finally he said, "You couldn't prove a thing."

His statement surprised her. He must know more about Paul than she'd given him credit for. "Would that make any difference as far as Anna is concerned?"

After another pause he said, "Perhaps not. But I can't believe you would want unsavory rumors about his father to get back to Rusty."

"What I want is for Rusty to have only good memories of Paul. But I'll fight for my son if I have to."

He grimaced and she saw a flash of pain in his eyes. "Ah, April, I'm sorry. I don't want any hard feelings between us. I know you have reason to resent the Dubois family. I know where Paul had been the night he died."

Her eyes widened. "You do?"

"I'd known about that woman for weeks. I asked him to stop seeing her. When you and Paul reconciled, I begged him to break off all communication with her."

She smiled sadly. "I could have told you not to waste your breath. It wasn't the first time, Noble, nor would it have been the last if Paul had lived."

He raised a hand as if he were preparing to fend off an attack. "I don't want to hear it, April."

It wasn't like Noble to take a what-I-don't-know-can't-hurt-me attitude. But, of course, this was Paul they were talking about, the son he had idolized. "I merely want you to be aware that there were other women in Paul's life. And there were even worse things than that in our relationship."

37

He looked at her with a mixture of alarm and grudging respect. "I think we understand each other, April. My main concern is that Anna must never know about Paul's indiscretions."

Sensing that she had tipped the scales in her favor, at least for the moment, April said, "She won't learn it from me as long as things continue as they are for Rusty and me."

"We're agreed then. Now what about letting us take him to Shangri-la?"

"I'll talk to him. If he wants to go, you may take him."

"Thank you," he said in a tone that sounded humble, although April didn't doubt for a moment that Noble would fight her for Rusty if he ever really thought she wasn't fulfilling her maternal obligations adequately. He got to his feet. "I'll go and say good night to my grandson before I leave. Good evening, April."

She went into the kitchen and put on a kettle of water for tea. Nan had been baking during the day, and the smell of spices hung in the air. April took a ginger cookie from the cookie jar and munched it while she waited for the water to boil. After Noble had left the apartment, Nan Mead joined April in the kitchen.

"I heated enough water for two cups, Nan," April said. "Is Rusty asleep?"

Nan, a plump, maternal woman in her late fifties, settled into a chair at the kitchen table. "He's dead to the world. He must have had quite a workout. I'm glad you were able to take him skating. I heard him telling his grandfather it was the most fun he's ever had."

April poured their tea and joined the housekeeper at the table. "Noble and Anna want to take Rusty out of town for a few days after Christmas. With Rusty gone, you could stay longer than the two days you planned to spend with your daughter in Kansas City."

"I won't deny I'd like that, but are you really going to let him go?"

"If he wants to," April said, sipping her tea. "Noble and I had a talk. I think we understand each other now."

"I've always thought he was a good man at heart," Nan conceded, "and Mrs. Dubois is a nice person too. I don't know why Paul turned out as he did." She darted a look at April. "I'm sorry. I've no right to say a thing like that."

"It's all right, Nan." Only Nan and Elana knew the full truth about what had gone on in April's marriage. April had confided in Elana because she had to have someone to talk to or go crazy. And Nan had lived in the house with them ever since Rusty was born. It had not been possible to hide Paul's cruelty from her when April had appeared at breakfast with bruises on more than one occasion. "I've never understood it either. I just learned that Noble knows more about Paul than I thought. I should have realized he's too shrewd to have remained completely oblivious to reality, even where Paul was concerned. He wants Anna to keep her illusions though."

Nan pursed her lips sympathetically. "It would probably kill her to find out the truth. She's such an innocent, you'd think she'd lived in a convent all her life."

"She very nearly has," April said. "Noble has always been overly protective. He makes all the decisions for both of them. I don't suppose Anna's ever written a check in her life. She thinks everyone lives on charge accounts."

"Must be nice," Nan mused, "never having to think about money and staying within a budget."

April shook her head. "I wouldn't trade places with Anna for all the money in the world. And neither would you. You're too independent to live with someone like Noble."

"That's the truth. Funny how somebody else's life can look so appealing from the outside."

"Ummm. The greener-grass syndrome. Well, about Rusty. I'll talk to him tomorrow and if he wants to go up to Shangri-la with his grandparents, why don't you plan to stay in Kansas City for a week."

"You won't mind being here alone?"

April laughed and left the table to get another cookie. "I'm a big girl, Nan. Besides, everyone needs some time alone occasionally."

As April had expected, Rusty was enthusiastic about going to Shangri-la with Noble and Anna. The resort provided a variety of activities for youngsters, and his grandparents tended to give him whatever he wanted. He would come back spoiled and expecting to continue getting his own way. It would take a few days for April to set him straight again. But that didn't worry her excessively. As the busy days before Christmas came and went, she found that the evenings in the apartment were long and too quiet with both Nan and Rusty gone. She even found herself thinking of Victor Leyland. Where was he? With Rosie? April felt restless.

She made the mistake of mentioning her restlessness to Elana and, before she realized what had happened, she was being recruited to help with the New Year's Eve party her friend was planning. Elana handed her a guest list for the party and started talking about the menu.

"But you always have your parties catered," April protested. "What do you need me for?"

"To help me supervise, silly. Not to mention the fact that you're an attractive, unattached woman. You'll perk up things for the men."

"I haven't been to a party in ages," April said, glancing absently at the long guest list. A couple of times a year Elana entertained clients and potential clients of her interior decorating firm, which had become quite successful. "I've never even heard of most of these people. I won't have anything to say to them."

Elana ran a hand through her blond hair and laughed. "Good Lord, April, you've been out of circulation too long. You sound like a sixteen-year-old contemplating her first date."

April shifted uncomfortably in her chair. "You didn't say anything about a date!"

Elana shook her head. "Don't panic. It was merely a figure of speech. I'm not trying to matchmake. I just want you to come to the party and be an unofficial co-hostess. You know, circulate and talk to people who seem to be left out. It'll be good for you."

"Oh, Elana, I don't know . . ."

"I'm counting on you, April."

Since she had no valid excuse for begging off, April reluctantly agreed.

After they had discussed the party at some length and Elana had gone, April even began to feel a bit of anticipation. She had had no social life since Paul's death. In fact, long before that she and Paul had stopped going out except for occasions when he felt their being seen together would bolster his image as a family man. Those occasions had been more endurance contests than enjoyable outings as far as April was concerned. Elana's party might actually be pleasant for her.

The next day she brought home a new dress from the boutique to wear to the party—a body-skimming silk charmeuse floor-length shift in winter white. The gown had a modest neckline and raglan sleeves with a slit to above the knee on one side of the narrow skirt. She dressed it up with touches of gold in glittering necklace chains of various lengths, a gold-link belt, and high-heeled sandals.

She stood before the full-length mirror in her bedroom on New Year's Eve and ran her eyes over her reflection. The dress that had looked modestly unrevealing on a hanger somehow took on a seductive aspect on April. She decided it was the way the supple material hugged her breasts, curving hips, and long, slender legs. The knowledge sent an excited little tingle along her veins that surprised her. On a sudden impulse her hands went to the hair confined sleekly in its neat chignon. She pulled out the pins and shook shining black waves loose to cascade over her shoulders.

Gazing at herself in some amazement, she realized that her boutique customers might not recognize her if they saw her this way. She felt rather as if she were wearing a disguise. Then she smiled at this fanciful thought. "Elana is right," she muttered. "You've been hibernating too long, old girl." She was merely going to help Elana with her party, meet a few people, chat about the weather and holiday activities, and come home alone. Only someone whose life was confined to home and the boutique could feel the slightest anticipation about the prospect. She turned quickly away from the glass, scooped up the small gold clutch lying on her bed, and left the apartment.

Elana herself answered the bell. Unaware of the breathtaking picture she presented framed in the doorway, April smiled perplexedly. "Why are you staring at me like that? I'm your friend, remember? You invited me."

"Wow!" Elana exclaimed. "You're a knockout in that dress. I'm positively green!"

"It's a nice holidayish color."

Elana made a face at her.

April looked uncertain. "Is the dress really all right?"

Elana reached out and pulled her into the apartment. "It's perfect." She led April into a crush of laughing, talking people, lifted a glass of champagne from the tray of a passing waiter, and placed it in April's hand. "Jerry, I want you to meet someone."

A sandy-haired man of about forty who had been talking with a young couple turned at the sound of his name. He smiled distractedly at Elana, the smile warming noticeably as his eyes fell on April. "Jerry Baker, this is my friend and neighbor, April Dubois. Jerry owns a floor-covering manufacturing company. We've worked together on several jobs."

"She charms me into selling to her wholesale," Jerry said, his gray eyes studying April interestedly.

"Don't you believe it," Elana responded. "If he didn't make such fabulous carpets, I wouldn't think of paying the exorbitant prices he charges. Wholesale, ha! Well, I'd better check the canape table."

"What can I do to help you?" April said quickly.

"Everything's under control. Just circulate. Jerry, introduce her to some people, will you?"

"It'll be my pleasure." Jerry made good on his word by introducing her to the couple with whom he had been talking before Elana interrupted. They were Ed and Bonnie Kline. Ed was a distant cousin of Elana's.

Jerry, it turned out, had been recently widowed and, upon learning of April's similar status, seemed to feel they had a great deal in common. He stayed at her side, steering her from one cluster of guests to another. When he hinted that he would like to take her to dinner later in the week, she found an opportunity to extricate herself and made her way to the far side of the room and the canape table.

She put a few tidbits on a crystal plate and swept the room with a glance. Her eyes jolted to a stop on the man standing near one of the long balcony windows. He wore staid evening black and white but there was nothing staid about his bold wink when he saw her. Victor Leyland! What was he doing here? She hadn't seen his name on the guest list.

The appraising look he was giving her brought back a sharp memory of the way he had leaned across the counter at the boutique to bring his face close to hers.

He raised his champagne glass to her in a mocking salute.

She turned abruptly away from his look, caught sight of an elderly, white-haired woman standing a few feet away, and introduced herself.

A buffet supper was served at midnight. By that time April had met and talked to several of the guests and had received three invitations to sit at particular tables. Victor Leyland had not sought her out. She was disappointed and trying to deny it to herself. She decided to join the Klines and Bonnie's sister, who was visiting from California. In spite of firm resolutions, she found her gaze, again and again, seeking out Victor Leyland. To her embarrassment, every time she found him his steady gaze snagged hers before she could shift it to something else and pretend not to notice him.

She mused unhappily that she was making rather a spectacle of herself. She felt certain he must be accustomed to women taking an interest in him. He couldn't have come to the party alone, although she had seen no buxom redhead among the guests. Maybe he was seeing somebody besides Rosie now. At any rate, he seemed to find her covert glances amusing. She was glad when the meal was finished; by that time it was late enough to take her leave without seeming rude. Leaving the table, she headed for the kitchen in search of Elana.

Finding no one in the kitchen, she called her friend's name and turned down a narrow hall that led to a pantry and on to the bedrooms. Victor Leyland emerged into the hall at the same moment and they very nearly collided. His big hands clasped her arms to steady her.

"Oh, I'm sorry," she stammered, feeling like a fool.

"I'm not."

She shifted uncomfortably. "I was looking for Elana."

"She's showing one of the guests to a bedroom. The lady had too much champagne." The warmth of his fingers on the inside of her wrist made her skin tingle. The corners of his well-shaped mouth lifted slightly, as if at some private joke. His blue eyes slid over her face like a caress, and she felt an erratic leap of her pulse. He was standing too close to her, still grasping her wrist lightly. Her eyes were wide with apprehension.

She wanted to step back, but somehow she couldn't move. His thumb stroked the tender skin of her wrist. "I'm not letting you get away this time until I learn your first name."

She tried to clear her dazed senses. "It's April."

"April," he repeated with mocking narrow-eyed insight. "You're the owner of the boutique?"

"Yes," she admitted.

"You might have told me that when I was there and saved me from making an idiot of myself."

"I—didn't think I'd ever see you again." She looked down self-consciously, staring studiously at his black shoes. Finally she said, "Have you known Elana long?"

"Several months. She redecorated the—building where I have an office. And you? How long have you known her?"

"For years. We were roommates at college." The narrow hallway suddenly seemed too small. Victor Leyland's solid form took up most of the available space and April felt, all at once, as if she couldn't get enough air. "I wanted to say good night to her, but I'll wait for her in the kitchen." She started to move away from him and felt the merest tugging on her wrist as he turned her back to face him.

He looked up toward the ceiling. She followed his gaze and saw a piece of mistletoe hanging over the doorway. When his gaze lowered to meet hers again, her eyes blinked closed of their own volition. Then she felt his thumb stroking gently across her quivering bottom lip. Her eyes blinked open, and she was dizzied by the way his gaze wandered intently over her features.

Almost hesitantly he bent his head and brushed his lips across hers. A small sigh escaped her parted lips. Instinctively she moved closer. Inwardly she was quaking like a tiny leaf in a fierce wind.

For a long moment his lips continued to brush and taste lightly. Their bodies touched, and then, as if he had been waiting since their last meeting for this moment, he

46

clutched her to him. His mouth melded to hers, a smoldering fire in it.

April swayed toward him as his mouth moved over hers, savoring her taste. His tongue sliding persuasively past her teeth jolted her into the realization of what was happening.

I can't, she thought with sudden panic, and then she felt the tentative, sensuous probing of his tongue against her own, taking pleasure and giving it. His mouth plundered hers until something hot and primitive erupted inside her. Terrified of her reaction, shamed by what she was allowing to happen, she lifted her shaking hands and pushed against his chest. The gesture was pitifully weak against the solid bulk of his body, and he didn't budge. But he lifted his head, reluctantly breaking the kiss. For a long, throbbing moment, they stared at each other.

April covered her trembling mouth with her hand. Victor loosened his hold on her, but continued to grip her shoulders lightly as his blue eyes searched her face. She was flooded by his overpowering maleness, the nerve endings all over her skin supersensitive. She couldn't think how to handle such an amazing situation. She had never been kissed by a stranger before, and a part of her was insulted and wanted to put him in his place. But another part sensed something solemn and frighteningly fated in what had happened. And she *had* been standing under the mistletoe. Any other woman would accept the kiss as a little lighthearted holiday reveling and think no more about it.

Confused, she looked away from him and muttered something about seeing Elana later. She walked into the kitchen, where she sagged weakly against a counter and buried her face in her hands for a moment, trying to

47

regain her composure. She had to get out of there before she made a total fool of herself. After a moment she slipped through the crowded living room, where liquor was flowing and hilarity was rising, retrieved her clutch bag from the entry closet, and let herself out. She would talk to Elana tomorrow.

Almost immediately she heard heavy footsteps muffled in the carpeting behind her. She glanced over her shoulder to see Victor Leyland, still getting into his overcoat, bearing down upon her.

"Did you come to the party alone?" he asked as he reached her.

"Yes," she answered primly, looking ahead.

"You're leaving rather early. Didn't you enjoy it?"

"Parts of it." She quickened her pace.

"I see." She darted a quick glance up at him and saw a wry smile slant his mouth. "I don't think I'll ask which parts. I'm not sure my ego could stand it."

"I have the feeling your ego can stand almost anything."

He chuckled. "And here I'd convinced myself I'd bowled you over with my charm." He studied her profile, his blue eyes dancing. "You aren't bowled over?"

Perhaps she had read too much into what had happened. He certainly seemed lighthearted about it all. She couldn't help smiling. "Not exactly."

"I'll have to try harder."

She looked at him sharply, her earlier apprehension returning.

"You shouldn't be out alone at this time of night. You don't even have a coat. My car's outside. May I take you home?"

Having reached the safety of her own apartment, April

experienced an impish flash. "Thank you just the same, Mr. Leyland, but I am home." She slipped her key into the lock, turned it, and stepped inside. "Good night," she said softly as she closed the door firmly and shot the bolt.

CHAPTER THREE

Elana appeared at April's door at three o'clock the next afternoon. In faded jeans and an old khaki shirt, her blond hair a haphazard tumble, her face devoid of makeup, Elana had clearly not been up long.

"I just discovered I'm out of coffee," Elana muttered, grimacing. "And there are munchkins in my head with hammers."

April grinned. "You shouldn't throw such wild parties. But I'll take pity on you. Coffee's already made."

Elana followed her to the kitchen, a cheery room equipped with warm fruitwood cabinets and a stainless steel sink and appliances. The cream wallpaper was dotted with plump strawberries, the floor tiled with a red and cream pattern. Elana lowered herself carefully into a chair. "I took three aspirin, but I can't tell it's helped much."

April surveyed her friend sympathetically. "How much did you have to drink anyway?"

"Not much. But champagne always does this to me."

April's dark brows lifted. "It's pretty dumb to drink it then, isn't it?"

Elana groaned. "Please, no lectures." Her eyes skimmed over April, who wore a gray sweat shirt and pants and running shoes, her black hair confined neatly in a single, thick braid down her back. "Must you look so

51

blasted chipper? Don't tell me you're actually going to run today."

"I thought I'd do a quick three miles. I want to start the new year right. You ought to try it. Does wonders for your state of mind, not to mention your figure." April had started running five months earlier, after moving into the apartment and discovering that a jogging track passed less than a block from the complex, following the course of Riverside Drive. It had done far more for her anxiety and depression than the tranquilizers her doctor had prescribed during the custody trial. She had been trying to talk Elana into joining her ever since, but to no avail.

Now Elana groaned again. "Just pour the coffee and forget the pep talk. I'll never understand why runners try to convert everyone in sight. Must be a case of misery loving company."

April laughed and carried two beige ironstone mugs to the table. "Would you like a Danish or a scrambled egg?"

Elana sipped her coffee gingerly to test the temperature, then swallowed more. "I don't want to think about food, if you don't mind. Listen, don't let me keep you from your disgusting physical workout. I can let myself out after I finish off three or four cups of this life-saving elixir."

"I'm in no hurry. I'm glad to have your company. Thank goodness Rusty's coming home tomorrow. I miss him."

Elana eyed her glumly. "How come you took a powder so early last night?"

"It was after one. I don't call that early. I looked for you to say good-bye, but I couldn't find you."

"Jerry was disappointed when he discovered you'd gone."

"Jerry Baker? The carpet maker?" April smiled at the unintentional rhyme, then she gave Elana a suspicious look. "You sly creature! You *were* trying to matchmake! You didn't need my help with the party at all. You wanted me to meet Jerry Baker."

Elana shrugged. "He's a sweet guy, April, if you'd give yourself a chance to get to know him."

"Thanks, but no thanks."

"I only thought—well, he's alone and so are you. You don't have to marry him, for gosh sakes! Just go out with him."

"No, Elana," April said firmly. "I'm sure Jerry Baker is a nice man, but I'm not interested. I have Rusty and the boutique, and I'm not looking for anything else."

"You can't live the rest of your life as you have the past year."

"Why not? I'm content."

"You can't be! Listen, kiddo, you can't let one bad experience turn you off the whole male population. If you don't care for Jerry, I have other friends. . . ."

"I met a few of them last night," April commented wryly.

Elana studied her thoughtfully. "Anybody in particular?"

"Well, I did receive a couple of dinner invitations, which I turned down. One of the men who asked me was married. He didn't even bother to take off his ring. Can you believe it? Then Victor Leyland . . ." She faltered. She had started to mention that kiss under the mistletoe, but somehow she couldn't share that moment, even with Elana. "He wanted to take me home."

53

"Victor Leyland?" Elana was staring at her. "Good Lord, you have fantastic luck. Well, what did you say? Did you let him bring you home?"

"I didn't let him, he followed me. He cautioned me about being out alone at night and offered to drive me. About that time we reached my apartment. I opened my door and left him standing there." She smiled, remembering Victor Leyland's startled look as she had shut the door in his face.

Elana made a helpless gesture. "I can't believe I'm hearing this. Don't you know who Vic Leyland is?"

April shook her head. "The name sounds familiar, but I can't think of where I've heard it before. He said you redecorated the building where he works. Maybe I've heard you mention him."

"He owns the building, all ten floors of it!" At April's still puzzled look, Elana sighed with exasperation. "The Leyland Building. You can't be downtown every day without having seen it many times." In fact, the Leyland Building sat next to the Williams Plaza Hotel. April saw the name carved into the stone façade practically every day. She felt foolish for not having made the connection.

"Oh, that Leyland."

"Yes, that one. My gosh, April, Vic Leyland is practically the most eligible bachelor in the state. He's made a fortune in the oil business since he left college ten years ago. I didn't really expect him to show up last night. I sent him a last minute invitation—I didn't even know he was in town until a few days ago. He'd been in Mexico on business for weeks."

That explained Victor Leyland's deep tan, April thought.

"When he arrived last night," Elana went on, "I figured he'd hang around for a half hour and go on to another party." She frowned. "Come to think of it, he might have come with Helen Frazier. I saw him talking to her several times. Helen overindulged in the bubbly and had to go to bed."

"Well, he didn't leave with her. Did she spend the night at your place?"

"No, somebody took her home about three."

April refilled her friend's empty mug. "Vic Leyland doesn't sound like any great shakes to me if he could walk out and leave behind the woman he came with."

Elana waved this observation aside. "Oh, you'd have to know Helen to understand. She makes a habit of going somewhere with one man and leaving with another. Besides, I'm not even sure they came together. If they did, they must have had an understanding to leave separately. Vic's too considerate to leave a woman in the lurch, even Helen Frazier."

"Considerate! I wouldn't call anyone who takes liberties with strangers—" She halted, blushing.

Elana was looking at her with great interest. "Liberties? What did he do? Come on, April, give. What happened between you and Vic Leyland?"

"Nothing." April laughed nervously. "It was merely the way he talked, as if he assumed I'd jump at the chance to let him take me home. He was entirely too familiar."

Elana laughed. "You're impossible. Any other woman *would* have jumped at the chance. I certainly would have."

"He was only amusing himself at my expense."

"Maybe he'll call you."

"I haven't the slightest interest in seeing him again,"

55

April said, wishing that she felt as sure of that as she sounded. "I don't want a man anywhere in my life, especially not someone like this Vic Leyland."

April was not even aware how much she gave away by that last phrase. She did know that a trivial New Year's Eve kiss, which should have been a meaningless incident, had, for her, been fraught with dangerously treacherous depths that she had no wish to plumb. The mere thought frightened her. She realized that her reaction was out of all proportion to what had happened. But that didn't make her feel any less troubled when she thought about it. However, she didn't intend to spend any more time thinking about Victor Leyland. She changed the subject abruptly, leading Elana to talk about the decorating jobs she had lined up for the weeks ahead.

A half hour later, when Elana went home, April left her apartment and ran across Riverside Drive to the jogging track. Her wish to start the new year off right was shared by a number of other joggers who passed her in the course of her run. Most of them were regulars on that particular track and, as was the custom, she exchanged friendly greetings with them as she jogged past.

The snow that had fallen before Christmas was gone now. Two unseasonably warm days had banished the last traces and the track was bare and dry, the occasional pothole clearly exposed. On the west, a chill, whitish mist from the river lingered in patches. The water was silvery between its sandy banks, rippling sluggishly downstream. The sky glowed faintly, neither gray nor white, but some unnamed color in between. The sun's last rays had that muted haze that sometimes came in the final moments before its setting. The vague euphoria that running provided seeped into April, and she gave herself up to it.

The early winter darkness was already closing in when she returned to her apartment building. Panting and perspiring, she turned a corner in the corridor and stopped short. Victor Leyland, wearing tweed trousers, a burgundy crew-necked sweater, and a chocolate brown leather jacket, lounged against her door.

She walked slowly toward him, feigning nonchalance. She almost smiled when she realized what a contrast her present appearance must have made to the way she had looked the night before. Let him see her at her worst, she thought. Perhaps the encounter was fortuitous after all. He would probably beat a hasty retreat after catching her in her old sweats and her hair escaping from its braid in wayward strands. The thought eased the tight feeling in her chest.

"Well, Mr. Leyland, did you lose something around here last night?"

His blue eyes ran over her, from head to toe and back again. "In a manner of speaking."

She paused awkwardly in front of the door, her key chain dangling from her cold fingers. "What was it?"

He stepped away from the door so that she could unlock it. "It may take some time to explain. I could tell you more comfortably over dinner."

"Sorry, but that won't be possible." She opened the door and turned to face him on the threshold.

"Do you have other plans?"

"Yes."

"Are you going out?"

"No, I plan to stay here and enjoy a quiet evening. I have to go back to work tomorrow. My housekeeper and my son will be home tomorrow as well." Maybe the mention of Rusty would give him pause.

It didn't. "We could phone for pizza if you don't feel like cooking. I'm very easy to please." He gave her a crooked smile filled with male allure.

Easy to please. He had said the same thing about Rosie. Maybe Rosie was a good influence. "Really, Mr. Leyland, what are you trying to accomplish here?"

He chuckled. "I should think that would be obvious." She'd said the same thing to him at the boutique. Was he mocking her? "But let me come in and we'll talk about it."

She wanted to invite him in, she realized. The knowledge would bear investigation later on. Right now she was beginning to feel a little silly, standing there.

He seemed to sense her hesitation. "I won't overstay my welcome, I promise you."

If she let herself, she thought in alarm, she could positively bask in his presence. Her reaction to him confused her. "All right, come in."

She showed him into the living room. "You can wait here while I get out of my running clothes, Mr. Leyland. There's coffee in a pot in the kitchen if you want a cup."

He made a wry face. "It's Vic, April."

She looked up at him and wondered suddenly if she should have let him come in. "Vic, then . . ."

His expression was amused. "Thank you."

She turned away from his intent regard. "The phone's in the hall if you want to order pizza," she said as she left the room.

Standing under the hot shower spray a few minutes later, she thought about Vic Leyland's presence in her living room and wondered if she could have dreamed the encounter. She couldn't believe she had actually let him come in. He did have a way of worming his way past a

58

person's defenses. It wasn't that she was afraid of him. After all, Elana knew him, so he must be all right. It was just that he represented something she wanted no part of. At least, she had thought she wanted no part of it until two weeks ago.

After drying herself, she dressed in slim camel-colored corduroy jeans and a bulky navy sweater. She brushed her hair out hurriedly and secured it in a loose bun atop her head. She put on no makeup except for a dash of lip gloss.

When she entered the living room, she saw that Vic had removed his jacket and was sprawled on the sofa, a coffee mug in one hand. He appeared quite large and dark against the delicate sapphire and champagne of the room. "I ordered one pepperoni and one hamburger," he informed her. "I forgot to ask what kind you liked before you got into the shower. I considered sticking my head in to ask, but I thought better of it."

"It's a good thing you did!" She found herself returning his smile. "Pepperoni's fine."

He finished his coffee and set the mug on a lamp table. "I had in mind something a little classier for our first date," he observed.

Her eyes were large, dark, and uncertain. "I don't consider this a date, Vic. I really can't imagine what you're doing here anyway. From what Elana has told me, your time must be valuable."

To her dismay she found that she was staring at his firm, sensuous lips. As she watched he smiled ruefully. "So that's it. What has Elana said to make you distrust me?"

"No, it isn't that," she said hastily. "Elana said very little, and that was complimentary."

59

He looked at her thoughtfully for a moment. "Are you involved with someone else?"

"No!" The word was abrupt, a message that she resented his questions.

But he didn't heed the message. "You've been a widow for a year now."

She stared at him. "How do you know how long I've been widowed? Have you talked to Elana about me?"

He shook his head. "I didn't have to. I knew Paul slightly. It didn't register with me who you were until after I got home last night. Dubois is not a common name."

Hearing that he had known Paul made her warier than ever. "How did you know my husband?"

"I'm a member at Southern Hills. I played golf with him a few times. As I say, I was only slightly acquainted with him. He seemed a nice enough guy, but he's dead." Somehow she knew that he was being deliberately blunt, trying to shake her into accepting the fact that she would never see her husband again. He thought she was still grieving for Paul. If he only knew! "Isn't it time you started to live again?" he queried softly.

"I have a good life, Vic—the boutique and my son. I made up my mind, when Paul died, that I didn't want anything more."

His expression was disbelieving. "You can't really mean that."

She sat down in a chair and regarded him solemnly. "I do."

He eyed her sharply. "Why? It doesn't make sense."

"It's a long story."

"I've got hours."

"Well, I'm not going to bore you with the details of my

60

life. I'll just say that my marriage left me leery of entanglements."

"Because your marriage was so good you don't think it can happen again? Or because it was so bad you aren't willing to risk getting involved a second time?" He remembered the fleeting sadness he'd seen in her eyes at the boutique and he thought he knew the answer.

She looked down at her hands clasped in her lap without replying. The sound of the doorbell jarred into the stillness. Vic sprang to his feet. "Must be the pizza." He went to the door to pay the delivery boy, then carried the food into the living room. "Where should I put this?"

She stood. "In the kitchen. I'll make fresh coffee. Or would you prefer cola?"

He followed her into the kitchen and set the pizza box on the table. "Cola, please."

When she carried two glasses to the table, he was finishing off a piece of the hamburger pizza. "Ummm. Nobody can make pizza like Shotgum Sam."

After the briefest hesitation she sat down. She lifted a triangle of pepperoni pizza and took a warm, savory bite. Strings of melted cheese dangled from her mouth, and she licked her lips to capture them, unaware of the sensuous nature of the action. She glanced across the table at Vic. His eyes were riveted on her lips. The silence between them was suddenly rife with electricity.

"I—I guess I'm hungrier than I thought," she confessed. She applied herself to the pizza, profoundly conscious of his eyes on her. What in the world was wrong with her? The only way to eat pizza was with the hands. She'd never felt self-conscious about it before. But then, her mind whispered, you've never eaten pizza with Vic Leyland before.

She was absurdly aware of the faint sound of the kitchen clock ticking. "So . . ." he said huskily, as if he were rousing from a daydream. He picked up a third wedge. "You own the boutique. Is it something you got into after Paul's death?"

She looked up at him, grateful that he wasn't going to return to questioning her about her marriage. "I opened it last March. It's doing well enough to keep me very busy."

His blue eyes considered her. "No one can work all the time. I run a good-size business myself, but I manage to keep my weekends and most evenings free."

"But you must have dozens of employees. I have only one full-time woman and a couple of part-time students to help me. When I do have free time, I spend it with Rusty."

When he didn't respond, she said, "You told me in the hall before that you lost something out there last night. What was it?"

He smiled. "The answers to some questions. You didn't give me a chance to ask them last night."

She took a steadying breath. "I don't want to talk about Paul or my marriage."

That stopped him for an instant. "Okay. How old is Rusty?"

"Six."

"He's in school then."

"First grade. He's been away for a few days with his grandparents, but he'll be back tomorrow."

He smiled. "So you said. I'd like to meet him."

Was he serious? "Why?"

He shrugged. "I like kids."

"You don't have children, do you?"

He shook his head. "I was married once, for two years, but we didn't have children. Dana didn't want any. I've been divorced for eight years, but I always planned to marry again someday."

"Helen Frazier?"

He seemed surprised. "Do you know Helen?"

"No, Elana told me she was the woman who had to go to bed at her place last night. She said she thought you brought Helen to the party. But you left without her. I imagine she's furious with you. So if you are planning to marry her, you'd better mend your fences quickly."

"You think I walked out on her?"

"Well . . ."

"I didn't. Helen and I have known each other since our school days. When she's between men I sometimes act as escort for her. We're friends, that's all. Last night she met someone who interested her and wanted him to take her home. She told me to go on without her." He finished the last wedge of pizza and sat back in his chair with a satisfied expression.

"What about Rosie?"

"Who?"

"The woman you bought the robe for."

He threw back his head and laughed. "Rosie Plimpton is my housekeeper. She's as wide as she is tall, and her heart's pure gold. She liked the robe, by the way."

"Oh . . . *oh!* At the boutique you deliberately let me think you were buying a gift for some woman you were involved with!"

His blue eyes twinkled mischievously. "You seemed so taken with the idea, I didn't have the heart to disillusion you. And don't forget, you weren't exactly forthcoming with me either."

An unexpected chuckle escaped her. "I guess we're even, aren't we?"

He leaned back in his chair. "Any other ladies in my life you'd like to know about?"

She raised an eyebrow. "How many others are there?"

"No more than a dozen or so."

"Great. I knew my first instinct was right. I should never have invited you in."

He got to his feet. "I can tell when I've worn out my welcome."

She had a sudden urge to ask him to stay longer, but she stifled it resolutely. At the door she said, "Good-bye, Vic."

"This isn't good-bye, April." He looked down at her as her eyes widened uncertainly. "I'll try not to push you faster than you're ready to go, but I have every intention of seeing you again."

Her eyes grew larger. "But I've tried to . . ."

"April," he said softly. Then with exquisite slowness he reached out and drew her against him, his eyes holding her gaze unwaveringly. He was giving her time to tell him to stop if she wanted, but she said nothing.

April simply lost herself in his eyes. She was achurn with conflicting emotions, unreasonable excitement, panic. When Vic pulled her trembling body tightly against his, she hadn't the strength nor the desire to pull away. She felt as if her bones had disintegrated, and mingled with the bewildering fear that was rising in her there was thankfulness for the support of his strong arms, for she doubted at that moment that her legs could have held her upright.

She became aware then of the intimate contact with the length of his body; it was rock-hard, unyielding, male, and burning with a heat that spoke of urgency and deep need. Her soft, feminine form seemed to melt against him like the wax of a burning candle clings to its sides.

She seemed incapable of tearing her gaze from his, and so her face was tilted up, her lips in perfect position when his mouth came down to claim them. The panic in her stirred again and for a moment she toyed with the thought of pushing him away. But the thought drifted off, and her lips parted. It was as if they had a will of their own that sought the warm delights that could be found in the probing insistence of his tongue. A shudder ran through her as his hands shaped and molded themselves to the contours of her hips, pulling her firmly against his lower body. She felt the masculine throbbing of his banked desire.

For timeless moments she couldn't control the hunger in her that responded to his sensual demand. But even as her arms crept up across his shoulders to wind around his neck, while her fingers laced themselves through the thick texture of his hair, alarm began to toll in some obscure corner of her brain.

Vic groaned and freed her mouth to explore the smooth ivory skin of her throat, sending chills along her nerves to the ends that quivered helplessly like exquisitely sensitive openings in her flesh.

As his mouth trailed hot fire across the soft hollow of her shoulder bone, she surfaced from her dazed state enough to murmur a small protest. "Vic . . ."

Vic's lips nibbled gently at her earlobe. But suddenly the deliciously warm tingles had been replaced by quivering fear. He wasn't hurting her, and yet the pain that Paul had inflicted on her in the past was pouring through her with so much intensity that for one horrified moment she imagined that it was Paul, and not Vic, who held her imprisoned in his arms.

At her strangled "No!" he paused, lifted his head, and looked down at her in confusion. She covered her face with her hands and pressed her forehead against his shoulder.

Her trembling communicated her distress to him, and his hands became exquisitely gentle, stroking down her back slowly, comfortingly, until she began to relax.

"It's all right, April," he whispered. He placed his hands on either side of her head and tilted her face so that he could look into her eyes. Troubled concern for her was clearing the mists of passion that had clouded his blue eyes. "I'm sorry. I don't know what I did wrong, but I'm sorry."

"It wasn't you," she murmured.

"Will you have dinner with me tomorrow night?"

Immediately her dismay returned. "I can't. It'll be Rusty's first night home."

"We'll take him with us."

Her brown eyes were huge and unhappy. "He—he wouldn't want to."

"Let him decide."

Before she could reply, he dropped a light kiss on her forehead and released her. He opened the door and turned back to say, "I'll check with you tomorrow." Then the door clicked shut behind him.

For a long moment April stared at the door, not seeing it, not seeing anything. Dazedly she turned back to her empty apartment.

* * *

66

As she lay in bed that night she relived those moments when she had responded to Vic so strongly. What if she hadn't come to her senses? Would she have let him go on, ravishing her senses, until neither of them could have turned back?

She could see that she had been too sure of her immunity to all men. It was frightening to learn that after all the years of unhappiness with Paul she was still vulnerable, given the right circumstances and the right man. Tonight she had submitted to the plundering temptation of Vic's mouth and body with very little effort to stop him—until the old familiar fear had flooded through her, reminding her of Paul and the dread with which she had come to anticipate his lovemaking. She must not allow herself to be maneuvered and coaxed into such a defenseless position again. No man would ever trap her as Paul had done, no matter how expertly he could evoke passion in her. Her freedom was too important to be exchanged for fleeting moments of sensual pleasure.

CHAPTER FOUR

"He's so persistent, Elana." April spooned blue cheese dressing on her chef's salad from a three-bowled server. Then she stared at the dressing and gasped, "Darn! I wanted Thousand Island. Oh, well . . ." She had phoned her friend that morning and invited her for lunch at a restaurant in the Forum. After what had happened the day before she needed a sympathetic ear. She peppered her salad, then grabbed her napkin and, turning her head aside, sneezed. "I've never known anyone quite like him. He rattles me."

From across the table Elana smiled. "I never would have guessed! You're so calm."

April reached for her fork, knocking her spoon onto the floor beneath the table in the process. "Honestly, I shouldn't even be here. We're having a post-holiday sale, and we were swamped all morning."

"I'll bet Val was glad to get rid of you for an hour. You're strung as tight as a guitar string. You've already salted your salad twice."

"I have?" April set the salt shaker down and gazed at her friend, unable to conceal the unwanted glimmer of misgiving in her eyes as she considered Elana's words. "You're supposed to be helping me!"

"What do you want me to say?" Elana asked, her gray eyes aglitter with amusement.

"I don't want you to say anything," April protested

69

with a small sigh as she forked a piece of lettuce and shook some of the salt off it. "Well, that isn't exactly true. I guess I want you to convince me that Vic Leyland is a rogue and I should stay away from him."

Elana grinned. She ate several spoonfuls of vegetable soup as she watched April fidget in her chair and toy with her salad. She put her spoon down and reached for a cracker. "You don't want me to lie, do you?"

"No," April sighed. Her lips curved wryly. "I already know what you think of Vic. Obviously he's charmed you into believing he's the greatest thing since sliced bread."

Elana munched a bite of cracker. "Charming you is what he seems to have on his mind at the moment."

"I can't figure out why he picked me."

"Oh, don't be so self-effacing."

"Well, he must know hordes of women who are more sophisticated and more willing than I."

"So you're a novelty. It's as valid a reason as any. You say he just showed up at your place yesterday unannounced?"

"He was waiting for me when I returned from jogging, and like an idiot I invited him to come in," April admitted, "and he ordered pizza, so he had to stay long enough to eat."

Elana smiled again. "Sounds cozy."

April groaned, picking through her salad as though in search of buried treasure. "That's what I'm so worried about. I mean, I sat there, eating pizza and feeling like a teenager again."

"Giddy, you mean? Like it felt when the football captain smiled at you in the hall. Or when the basketball star asked to borrow your classnotes. Gad, high school was torture."

April waved her fork for emphasis. "My point is that I'm too old for such silliness. Elana, you know what my marriage was like. When I was dating Paul I thought he was wonderful. I was totally blind to the clues to his character. All he had to do was kiss me and let sweet phrases roll off his tongue, and I forgot whatever doubts I had. Obviously I'm no judge of men!"

"Don't you think you're being too hard on yourself? You had a sheltered upbringing, and Paul was the first man you were ever serious about. You had nothing to judge by. You're older and wiser now."

April pointed her fork at Elana. "You'd better believe it! Wise enough to be cautious."

"There's a difference between caution and a refusal to trust any man, ever." Elana tapped her spoon against her coffee cup to accentuate her words. "You can't generalize from a single instance. Vic Leyland is nothing like Paul."

"How can you be sure? I mean, would you ever have guessed that Paul would be a wife-abuser? Good Lord, he was a real Dr. Jekyl and Mr. Hyde. Like a fool I got pregnant almost immediately, and then I felt trapped. Every time Paul had one of his blow-ups he was so apologetic and contrite when the storm was past. I wanted to believe his promises because I felt I should stay with him for Rusty's sake. When I finally did try to leave . . ."

"He took Rusty," Elana finished for her. "Look, April, I know you got a bad deal, the worst. But you can't let it color the rest of your life."

April shook her head firmly. "To keep my son I had to tuck my tail between my legs and ask to be allowed to come back. I'm not sure I could have stood it much longer, even for Rusty." She shuddered with the memory. "When Paul died I felt as though I'd been let out of jail. I swore that I would never let a man have power over me again. I didn't even want a man to get within ten feet of me."

"So why are you agonizing over whether to go to dinner with Vic tonight?" Elana asked, an impish gleam in her eyes.

April's mouth turned down in a grimace. "I honestly don't know. I think I've slipped a cog. Why didn't I give him a flat no yesterday?"

"Simple," said Elana, answering her own question as well as April's. "You like the guy, and you want to go out with him."

April laughed. "Am I insane, or what?"

"You're just a woman who's intrigued by an attractive man. It's perfectly natural. Why don't you relax and go with the flow?"

That was easy for Elana to say. She hadn't lived for years with a man who could be solicitous or cruel by turns, and there was no way of knowing on any given day which it would be. Elana hadn't come to dread her husband's slightest touch; she hadn't experienced the slow death of her sexual responses. She hadn't been told so many times that she was frigid that she had come to believe it.

"And will you put that fork down?" Elana added. "Before you stab somebody."

April looked at the fork in her hand as though she hadn't known it was there. Then she laid it down and met Elana's look. "If I do go to dinner with Vic tonight, I'm taking Rusty."

Elana's cracker halted halfway to her mouth. "Does Vic know that?"

"Actually he's the one who suggested it."

72

"I'll bet it was the only way he could get you to agree."

April shrugged. "Well, I don't want to leave Rusty on his first night home."

"Oh, come off it," said Elana deliberately, "you're taking him along as protection." She took a bite of the cracker, munching vigorously.

"What do you mean, protection?" April asked with a sudden frown.

"It's obvious, April. It's going to be difficult for Vic and you to get chummy with Rusty watching you. You and Vic are going to have a six-year-old chaperon."

"Well, I don't care." April pushed her uneaten salad aside and folded her hands on the table. "The last thing I want is to get chummy, as you so succinctly put it, with Vic Leyland. Why are you laughing?"

Elana smothered a giggle in her napkin. "I'm just wondering why you think you need a chaperon. Is it Vic or yourself you're afraid of?"

April was too busy during the afternoon to ponder Elana's question much. Determined to strike exactly the right tone of insouciance that evening, between customers she mentally considered and discarded most of the items in her wardrobe.

She drove home after work, grumbling to herself about men who were so pushy they wouldn't give a woman time to examine all angles of a situation. Her late father had had a saying: Get all your ducks in a row, April, before you make a decision. But Vic wasn't giving her time to get her ducks in a row.

She finally decided on a simple blue-and-black textured suit for dinner. Provided Vic called. She hadn't heard from him since yesterday. Maybe the idea of taking

73

Rusty along had paled in the meantime, and he had decided to forget dinner after all. Why that thought should cause a distinct sinking feeling in the pit of her stomach, April couldn't have said.

As she stepped into the apartment foyer, she heard laughter coming from the kitchen—Rusty's and Nan's. She left her coat in the foyer closet and went directly to the kitchen.

Rusty, Nan, and Vic were seated around the table drinking glasses of chocolate milk. Vic lounged back in his chair, one arm flung over its back. The offhand pose seemed at odds with his brown vested suit and shirt of pristine white. He held his half-full glass of milk in one hand. Rusty was on his knees in his chair, his elbows on the table, his chin in his hands. Nan's plump face was flushed with amusement. Both Nan and Rusty were listening raptly to Vic's tale about being thrown from a horse into a bed of cacti.

Nan saw April first. "Ah, here she is! Rusty, you run along and get your bath, in case . . . well, you know . . ."

Rusty scrambled out of his chair. "Hi, Mom! Vic's been telling us about when he got his first horse when he was eight. Did you know he's got dozens of horses on his ranch? And cows and a collie too!"

"No, I didn't know that." April slanted a look at Vic, and he grinned devilishly. In this well-lighted homey room his eyes looked as bright as sapphires. The gleam behind the thick lashes made her uneasy in a way that she was at a loss to describe. "What else has Vic been telling you?"

Rusty chuckled lustily. "The first time he got on his

horse, the horse bucked and threw him into his mother's cactus bed. He couldn't sit down for a week!"

"That's very funny, Rusty," April said, giving Vic a dry look. "I trust he's learned to ride better since then."

"Some," Vic said as he unwound himself from the chair back. "Did you have a hard day at the boutique?"

"It was mayhem."

"Poor dear," Nan said. She got up and wiped her hands on her white apron. "You just sit down there and I'll get you a nice cup of tea."

Rusty tugged at her sleeve. "Vic wants us to go to dinner with him. Can we, Mom?"

"Rusty, let your mother catch her breath," Nan scolded.

"Can we go to dinner with Vic, Mom?" Rusty repeated impatiently.

"Are you sure you aren't too tired for a night on the town?" April asked her son. "By the way, how was school today?"

"It was okay," Rusty said. "And I'm not too tired to go out with Vic."

"We'll have him back by eight," Vic said, mentioning the hour Rusty had informed him was his bedtime. "I made reservations at the Smuggler's Inn." April fingered her blouse collar nervously.

"Did you?" April asked innocently, shoving her hands into the side pockets of her wool skirt. "That was rather precipitate of you."

"Not at all," he contradicted. He hesitated, then added reluctantly, "Reservations can be canceled. Shall I cancel ours?"

"No!" Rusty exclaimed, jumping up and down. "We can go, can't we, Mom?"

She eyed Rusty thoughtfully, wondering how Vic had made a conquest of him so quickly. It must have been that story about the horse and the cactus bed. "I suppose so, if you'll hurry and get ready."

Rusty dashed from the room, turning at the door to say, "I'm going to wear my suit, like Vic."

Nan, who had been busy at the stove, set a cup of tea on the table. "I'll take this with me while I dress," April said. She glanced at Vic and her lip twitched. "Vic can entertain you with more stories of his reckless childhood."

But she was more concerned with his reckless adulthood, April told herself grimly as she stepped into the shower.

She emerged from her bedroom thirty minutes later to find Rusty and Vic waiting for her in the living room. "Well, finally," Rusty greeted her. "What took you so long?"

"There's something you have to learn about women, Rusty," Vic said. "They have to have a long time to make themselves beautiful before going out, although in your mother's case it's like gilding the lily."

April suppressed a smile. "You certainly know all the moves, Vic Leyland."

As he unfolded his lean height to stand, his almost overpowering maleness impressed itself upon April. There was a primal magnetism about him that was hard to define. His suit jacket swung open, revealing a close-fitting vest that emphasized his narrow waist and flat stomach. The brown slacks fell unwrinkled in two knife-sharp creases. Polished brown leather loafers gleamed beneath the bottom edge of the trousers.

"What's gilding the lily?" Rusty asked.

Vic caught April's gaze and held it. "It means that flowers are prettier in the garden as God made them than in vases," he said.

Rusty looked up at him, baffled. "Huh?"

Unaccountably April wondered if Vic was imagining her naked, as God made her. She glanced away. "I think he's saying he prefers a woman who looks—er, natural," she said.

"Right," Vic said, gripping Rusty's shoulder companionably. "Now, let's get out of here before this discussion deteriorates into total confusion."

Looking up at Vic as they left the apartment, Rusty said, "I've never been to the Smuggler's Inn before. I saw a movie about smugglers on TV. Do real smugglers go there?"

"If they do," Vic said, grinning, "they keep a mighty low profile. You couldn't tell a smuggler from the honest folks."

"Oh." Rusty sounded disappointed. "Do they have hot dogs?"

April groaned. Vic laughed and said, "I don't think so, but they make a great chicken fried steak."

Vic's car was a cedar-colored Eldorado with white leather seats. Rusty climbed willingly into the backseat, but he hung over the front seat between Vic and April all the way to the restaurant.

In a clear effort not to exclude Rusty, Vic said, "Before you came home Rusty was telling me how much fun he had with his grandparents at Shangri-la."

Turning sideways in her seat, April smoothed an unruly red lock on her son's forehead. "We didn't get to talk about it much last night, Rusty. You were so sleepy. Did you and Grandpa get to go fishing?"

"Yeah, at a heated dock. It was neat! You could fish right through a hole in the floor."

"Did you catch anything?"

"Sure, three perch and one bass. 'Course, the perch were too little to keep. But Grandma cooked the bass for my dinner."

"I'll bet it was delicious," April said. "Your grandmother is such a good cook."

"Yeah," Rusty agreed, "but I wish she didn't try to get me to sit on her lap all the time. And she's always huggin' and kissin' me and gettin' lipstick on my face. Yuck! I hate gooey kisses."

Vic was shaking with silent laughter. "Wait until you're sixteen," he commented.

"Rusty," April said hastily, "that's just Grandma's way of showing how much she loves you. I hope you didn't tell her how you felt about it."

"No, I didn't. . . . I didn't want to make her cry, but she did anyway."

April frowned, aware that Rusty was oblivious to the fact that he'd given away what Anna and Noble surely wanted kept secret, and uncertain how to deal with it. "Did Grandma cry while you were at Shangri-la?" April asked. Vic glanced at her with a studious expression, and she blushed. She was trying to pry information out of Rusty, but she wanted to know if Anna's crying had affected her son.

"Not at first," Rusty revealed, "but she cried a lot the last day we were there. She said it was because she was going to miss me when they brought me home. She cried in the car too."

"On the drive home?"

"Yes, and she said she wished I could live with her all

the time. I don't want to live with Grandma, Mom. I don't have to, do I?"

"No," April said emphatically, alarmed at this information. "Your home is with me."

Rusty expelled a deep breath. "Good. Hey, is that it?"

Vic had turned the Cadillac off the freeway. "This is it, chum," he said as he stopped in front of the restaurant and turned off the engine. "I'm hungry enough to eat a bear, fur and all, how about you?"

Rusty chuckled at Vic's grade-school humor. "Me too!"

Vic and April had lobster while Rusty had chicken fried steak and french fries. During dinner Vic chatted with Rusty with the ease of a man who was used to children. Vic's attention clearly raised him several notches in Rusty's estimation. April joined the conversation from time to time, but her thoughts kept going back to what Rusty had said about his grandmother. Anna's actions worried her. She knew that Anna still grieved for her only son, whom she had worshiped, but April couldn't allow her to put Rusty in Paul's place, if that's what Anna was trying to do.

"I have to go to the bathroom, Mom." Rusty was tugging on her jacket sleeve. April pulled her thoughts away from Anna and started to get up.

"You don't have to go with me," Rusty said, insulted. "I know where it is. I saw it when we came in."

April sank back into her chair. "Okay. Go ahead."

Vic watched Rusty walk away from the table. "Thank you for having the patience to talk to him," April said. "Most adults tend to ignore children when there are other adults around. You're very good with him. I'd swear you've had practice."

"I have two sisters," he told her. "Between them they've supplied me with six nieces and nephews. I see them as often as I can, which isn't often enough since they live in Omaha and San Diego." His eyes narrowed consideringly. "Want to tell me where you've been all evening?"

April smiled apologetically. "I'm sorry. I've been a good deal less than stimulating dinner companion, I know."

"I didn't say I'm not stimulated," he remarked in a velvety drawl. "And I'm not dense either. You've been brooding ever since Rusty dropped that information about his grandmother."

April leaned back in her chair, her shoulders sagging. "Do you blame me for being concerned?"

"No, but worrying about it will only give you ulcers. Tell Mrs. Dubois to cut out the histrionics."

April sighed. "I wish it were that easy. It wouldn't do any good to talk to Anna. She'd just be hurt. Maybe I should talk to Noble." She closed her eyes for a moment. "I don't relish that thought."

"Then don't allow them to see Rusty unless you're present."

She shook her head. "I don't think I could do that. You don't know Noble. He's—" She broke off as she realized that she was about to reveal more than she should.

"It's understandable that you'd be on guard with Noble Dubois," Vic observed. "From what I've heard, he didn't do you any favors at the custody trial."

She stifled a flush, terribly afraid for a moment that he knew of the picture painted of her by Paul's attorney—that of a frivolous, unstable woman who wasn't fit to

80

raise her child alone. No, he couldn't possibly know that. The courtroom had been closed to spectators. Noble had seen to that. All Vic could know was what was in the papers, a brief news item stating simply that Paul had been awarded custody of Rusty. But how had he known about Noble's testimony?

"I didn't expect him to take my side against his son's," she said.

He observed her thoughtfully. "I'd like you to tell me something about you and Paul. Were you still in love with him when you sued him for divorce?"

"That's a very personal question," she protested.

"I have very personal feelings about you, April. And since we met I've thought about Paul a great deal. I told you once that he seemed a nice enough guy, but it's fairly obvious that you were unhappy with him. I want to know who stopped loving whom, or was it a mutual drifting apart?"

"It was mutual," she managed weakly.

"So you went back to him after the custody trial to be with Rusty?"

"Yes."

He placed his arms on the table and leaned toward her. "Was that the only reason, April? Did you hope to win back his love? Did you share a bed? Did Paul's lovemaking excite you to the point of forgetting the problems in your marriage when you were in his arms?"

"That is none of your business!"

"When I hold you in my arms, April, I don't want another man to be in your head," he murmured.

"Then perhaps you shouldn't try to see me again," she retorted angrily. "Look, Vic, Rusty will be back any minute. I don't want him to hear us talking about his father."

"Were you still in love with Paul when he died?"

"No! But that doesn't mean I'm ready to fall into the arms of any man who comes along! I hope I make myself clear!"

He sighed. "Quite. . . . Here's Rusty now. Are you ready to go?"

When they got back to the apartment Nan supervised Rusty's bedtime routine, then retired to her own room. Sorry for her outburst in the restaurant, April invited Vic to stay for a brandy. They carried their snifters into the living room. April kicked off her high heels, removed her jacket, and curled into a corner of the couch. Vic took off his jacket and loosened his tie before he joined April on the couch.

Gazing into her brandy, April ran her index finger slowly around the rim of the snifter. The room was very quiet without Rusty's exuberance. As Vic settled himself comfortably next to her, his long legs thrust out in front of him, she realized that for the first time she felt relatively at ease with him. The tension between them had diminished during dinner and even though she had been defensive at the end and told him more about Paul than she had ever meant to, she couldn't help but feel flattered that a man like Vic Leyland should be interested in her. Not that anything could come of it. She would never be trapped in a relationship again! Dolefully she tried to snap out of the relaxed bemusement the brandy was weaving around her.

Vic sipped his brandy. "Deep thoughts again?" he inquired softly.

She leaned forward and set her snifter on the coffee table. Getting up, she said, "It's too quiet in here. I'll put some music on." She wandered over to the stereo player

82

and began looking through the tapes. "Do you like Mozart?"

Watching her, Vic said laconically, "Well enough."

She inserted the tape and the delicate strains of a piano sonata drifted through the room. She wandered back to the couch and sat down. She lifted her snifter, then thought better of it and replaced it on the coffee table.

"Am I making you nervous?"

April chewed her bottom lip self-consciously. Why couldn't she sit still? "Not at all! I—I'm worried about talking to Noble. He's so protective of Anna."

He bent forward slowly and set his snifter beside hers on the coffee table. "Do you think we could talk about something else besides your ex-in-laws?"

She stared at him, deeply aware of the movement of the muscles along his arm beneath the soft white fabric of his shirt sleeve. The sprinkling of dark hairs on the back of his extended hand, the flexing of the long fingers as he set the snifter down, sent an unaccountable tremor up her spine. She knew that she had better get control of the conversation quickly, or he would steer it into dangerously intimate channels.

"Tell me about you," she finally said. "You mentioned that you were married once. Was your wife a local woman?"

He straightened, turning a direct blue gaze upon her. "She was from Wichita. We met in college at O.U. We were both too young to make a lifetime commitment, and we married without really knowing each other. She wanted parties, trips, a jet-set style of living. I wanted a home and children. Fortunately we arrived at the conclusion simultaneously that it wasn't going to work. She went back to Wichita after the divorce."

He stated the bare facts as if he were telling her some-one else's story, as if he had no personal involvement in what he was saying. "Do you ever see her?"

"No." His blue eyes glimmered from beneath his dark lashes. "When something is dead it's best to bury it."

"Are you implying that I haven't . . ."

"Buried Paul?" he finished for her. "That may be put-ting it too strongly, but there was something in your mar-riage that still profoundly affects you. If you had been in love with Paul, I'd understand. As it is, I'm baffled."

April swallowed. "Some things are too personal to be talked about."

He studied her for a long moment. "Fair enough." Be-fore she comprehended what he was about, he reached out and began to take the pins from her hair, one by one, until the thick black waves tumbled over her shoulders. "That's what I wanted to do that day in the boutique," he said huskily. "And this." He combed his fingers through her hair, his hand coming to rest intimately at her nape. "We don't have to talk if you don't want to. I'd rather just look at you and touch you. Your skin is so soft, April. That Mona Lisa look in your beautiful eyes fascinates me. The faint dimple at the corner of your lovely mouth excites me. I want you, April. Ever since that first morning in the boutique I've been torturing my-self with visions of carrying you to bed and making love to you until you are wild beneath me."

April's dark eyes were huge with shock as, leaning to-ward her, he applied gentle pressure on the back of her head to urge her closer. Before she could assimilate his words completely or think of how to deflect him grace-fully, his mouth fused with hers in a kiss that galvanized every nerve in her body.

CHAPTER FIVE

It wasn't that she hadn't expected to be kissed. Vic had been looking at her all evening as though he wanted to kiss her. What she hadn't expected was her own willingness to let the kiss go on.

Maybe it was the brandy. Or maybe she was just getting to know Vic better. He smelled so good, an erotic mingling of clean skin and vibrantly scented aftershave. His arms around her were strong and warm, his chest a hard-muscled wall pressing against her breasts. Oddly, his body encircling her made her feel protected, as though she could let down her guard. Yet his kiss was becoming very aggressive.

She sighed as Vic's body pressed her into the comfortable angle of the couch, her head tilted back against the edge. His mouth was seeking and warm, and it tasted faintly of brandy.

It had been so long since she had been kissed by a man who wanted to give as much as he took. Years. And if she had ever been kissed like this, she couldn't remember. It was a new and bedazzling experience.

At that instant April couldn't have said why she wanted Vic to go on kissing her. She knew only that she was going to give in to the strange inquisitiveness that was skimming along the surface of her thoughts. For a little while she was going to experience Vic's kiss and her own curious reactions to it. Later she would draw back into her defensive shell before things got out of hand.

Vic's tongue dipped into her mouth, sending a small shock wave through her. Its texture was unexpectedly pleasing. Boldness seized her, and she acted on the impulse to explore his mouth, as he was exploring hers. With a moan too soft to be heard, she rested her hands in the crux of his shoulders and neck, curving her fingers close to feel the strong muscles bunched beneath his shirt. Slowly she ran her palms over his shoulders and back, feeling the ripple of well-toned muscles under her searching touch. From somewhere came the image of Vic's torso bared and her palms making contact with the smooth, tanned skin without the intrusion of his shirt. A thrill of excitement skipped through her.

She felt the deep thudding of Vic's heart as he crushed her closer. With a groan he released her mouth and his searing lips found the smooth, taut skin just below her jawline. Because her head was thrown back, resting against the couch, her throat was arched and exposed and he took full advantage of the delectable offering by pressing hot moist kisses down the line of her throat, hesitating at the hollow above her collarbone. His tongue searched the shallow cavity, delighting her senses with its sensuous probing.

His breath was hot on her skin as his mouth feathered kisses lower. He nuzzled into the V neckline of her crepe blouse, and a titillating shiver ran through her.

"Oh, Vic . . ." Could that be her voice? It sounded too throaty and cracked to be hers.

"God, April," he muttered hoarsely, "you are one beautiful woman."

Beautiful? She? April didn't think she was beautiful

but, at that moment, it thrilled her that Vic thought so. At that moment she could almost believe him.

Vic's hands glided slowly over the clinging crepe of her blouse from her shoulders across the curves of her breasts to meet at the top button. His fingers stilled for a moment, and he lifted his head to gaze into her heavy-lidded eyes. His own eyes, half hidden by the screen of his thick lashes, smoldered with passion. "You feel so good," he said hoarsely, "so good."

"Vic," she whispered as she wound her arms about his neck and threaded her fingers into the thick hair at the back of his head. "Vic, I . . ."

The words were muffled as his mouth traveled the distance between them to seal hers with a persuasive warmth that made her forget what she had started to say.

She tried to arrange her scattered thoughts into some coherent pattern. A dangerous languor had crept into her body, rendering her weak and pliant. How long had she been lying there, reveling in the renaissance of her senses? She had lost all account of time and place. She was losing her grip on reality. But as Vic's mouth moved hotly on hers she prevaricated, telling herself that she would take a few more minutes to languish in the ebb and flow of emotions that she had thought she would never feel again.

His tongue followed the shape of her soft, parted lips, repeating its journey until her fingers plowed deeper into his hair and a faint whimper escaped her. Oh, it was wonderful to feel like a woman again, to feel needed and wanted by a man.

The romantic strains of Mozart rippled around them. A groan emanated from deep in Vic's chest. His fingers loosed the first button of her blouse, traveled to the second button, and the third, releasing each in turn. When the last button was undone his hands went unerringly to the front clasp of her bra and deftly unfastened it, pushing it aside.

She gasped as her breasts fell into his hands to be cradled gently. Then his cupped palms covered her breasts and he palmed the rosy crests, rotating lightly until they tightened into thrusting nuggets.

When he bent to take an aching nub into his mouth, April began to tremble. She felt as if she were sinking into quicksand and was too weak to prevent it. Her head fell forward and came to rest against Vic's shoulder, her hair a tumbled disarray of black silk about her face. Her fingernails bit into the lean muscles at the small of his back.

The gentle tugging of his mouth sent off an answering throb deep inside her. It was then that it finally dawned on her that she had stepped willingly into a very dangerous situation.

"Vic? This is happening too fast. I have to think, please . . ."

"April, ah, April, I ache so for you."

He blazed a trail of kisses over the curve of her breast and up her throat to the sensitive spot just below her ear. A helpless incoherency escaped her as he laced his fingers through her hair, cradling her head in his hands. He kissed her heavy eyelids closed.

"Oh, Vic! I never meant . . . I don't want to feel this way . . . so out of control . . ."

"Let it happen," he whispered, and he kissed one corner of her trembling mouth and then the other before his lips covered hers completely. He drank of her taste, moving his mouth seductively back and forth on hers while he removed his tie and shirt. Then, crushing her soft breasts against his naked chest, he fell back on the couch, pulling her down beside him.

The coarse dark hairs on his chest abraded her breasts, tantalizing her senses. She lay in his arms and looked into his eyes and felt mesmerized by their blue depths and the adoration she saw there. He slid his hand down her back and over the curve of her hip and pressed her hard against him, leaving her no doubt as to his need.

The soft music from the stereo drifted to a stop, and the room was silent except for the sounds of their quickened breathing. With the abrupt stillness it seemed to April that nature held its breath and the world stopped turning for an instant. His eyes held hers captive. "I want to finish undressing you. I want you to undress me. I want to see your beautiful body in the lamplight and I want to feel all of you beneath me." While he spoke quietly his hand made a caressing journey over her hips and came to rest at the small of her back. "I want to make love to you, April."

Suddenly her throat ached, and she lowered her eyes. He tucked her head underneath his chin, smoothing her hair back in an exquisitely tender gesture.

"Vic, please . . ."

"What's wrong?"

"I just can't."

His hand continued to smooth back her hair, but she felt his body tense. "I know that you want me," he ventured.

"You make it sound so simple," she whispered miserably, "but it isn't."

"Why isn't it?"

"Maybe I'll tell you someday. I can't now."

His hand grew still, and there was a long silence between them. Then he levered himself into a sitting position and bent to pick up her blouse from the floor. He handed it to her without looking at her. His hand was unsteady. She sat up and slipped it on, hating herself and the situation that she had helped to create. Buttoning the blouse, she said in a voice thick with unshed tears, "I'm sorry."

He turned to look at her then. "Not nearly as sorry as I am," he said with a wry twist of his lips. He took a deep breath, as if he were fighting for control. "Damn it, April! I don't understand you."

She lifted her chin. "You're better off."

He stared at her lovely profile and shook his head. "What the hell does that mean?"

"Nothing."

Vic wanted to shake her, and he would have if he had thought it would do any good. But she had withdrawn from him. He could hardly believe that the pale, tense woman beside him was the same woman who had caught fire in his arms only minutes before.

Grunting, he reached for his shirt and put it on. Then he stood and put on his jacket, stuffing his tie into a pocket and dangling the vest in one hand.

He stood over her, and she felt humiliation and a stab of anger at the deliberative way he was looking at her. "I'm sorry you wasted your evening," she snapped.

"Don't, April," he sighed, and then he bent swiftly, grasped her chin, and planted a quick hot kiss on her mouth. He lifted his head and looked deeply into her eyes for a moment. "I wish you trusted me enough to talk to me."

After Vic had left the apartment April sat where he

had left her for several minutes. A few silent tears tracked down her cheeks as she tried to figure out how she could have forgotten herself to the extent of allowing things to progress as far as they had.

It had to be the newness of the experience for her. She had never responded to Paul's lovemaking as she had to Vic's, not even in the first weeks of their marriage before she began to get a glimmer of the kind of man she had married. Vic Leyland touched something elementally feminine in her. She knew in that moment that she could fall in love with him, and for that reason he was a threat to her.

Never again, she thought desperately. Love, in its own way, could be as strong a trap as fear, perhaps even stronger. She would be an idiot to give Vic that kind of power over her. But as she turned out the lights and went to bed, she couldn't shake the apprehension that he had already managed to get a hold on her.

"Who is Vic?" Noble Dubois stood in the center of the living room, his silvered red hair rumpled from playing with Rusty. His hands were thrust deep into the pockets of his gray trousers. The matching gray jacket was folded over the arm of the sofa, along with his topcoat.

April had walked into the apartment five minutes earlier and found Noble and Rusty sitting on the living room carpet, playing with Rusty's toy race cars and track. She'd been trying to catch Noble at his office for several days, had left messages, but he hadn't returned her calls. Now he had appeared at the apartment unannounced, when she would have preferred saying what she had to say to him at his office.

She had kissed Rusty and, promising he could come back in a few minutes, sent him from the room.

April's dark eyes narrowed. "I've been trying to get in touch with you for days. Why haven't you returned my calls?"

"I was out of town. I just got back to the office today. I cleared off my desk, then decided to come over here rather than phone."

And pump Rusty about what his mother had been up to, it seemed. It was too warm in the room. April took off her red suit jacket before she sat down in the armchair and smoothed the jacket across her knees. "How long have you been here?"

"An hour." Noble withdrew his hands from his pockets and lowered himself to the couch. He sat forward on the edge as if he were too tense to lean back and relax against the soft cushions. "And all I've heard about is some person named Vic. He seems to have made a big impression on Rusty. Who is he?"

Her father-in-law's proprietary attitude irritated April. She owed Noble no explanations for the company she kept. Besides, she hadn't heard from Vic since the evening he had taken her and Rusty to the Smuggler's Inn. When two days had passed and he hadn't called, she had decided that he wasn't going to. She had been telling herself ever since that it was for the best.

"Victor Leyland took Rusty and me to dinner the other evening."

Noble scowled, his thick brows lowering and dipping together over his nose. Plainly her statement had taken him by surprise. He knew Vic, of course. They'd served on some of the same boards and committees. "I wasn't aware that you knew Victor Leyland."

He obviously wanted to know how long and how well she had known Vic. She hated being put on the defensive; and she had no intention of discussing Vic with Noble.

"April," Noble said with gravity, "I know you must be lonely, but I hope you won't make any foolish choices on that account. Whatever decisions you make are going to affect Rusty as well as yourself. You must remember that." He spoke in the same slow, reasoning tone that she had heard him use with his wife. It was the tone adults often used with recalcitrant children.

She clasped her hands in her lap and met Noble's look squarely, determined not to let him see how resentful she felt. "I'm not in the habit of making hasty decisions, Noble. I believe I've proved that since I married Paul."

He regarded her with narrowed eyes, his head tilted back slightly. She knew that he was trying to judge the extent of her annoyance, to decide whether he could question her further about Vic. She said quickly, "I telephoned you because I want to talk about Anna."

Noble's expression changed from shrewd calculation to guardedness. "What about Anna?"

"I'm worried about her emotional state, Noble. She's becoming obsessed with Rusty."

"Now, April, *obsessed* is a pretty strong word." He spread his hands flat on either side of him on the sofa curiously, as if he didn't know what else to do with them. She had rarely seen Noble in a situation where he wasn't in command, but at the moment he seemed not only restless but uneasy. She had evidently touched a nerve.

"Rusty told me that she held him and cried when you were at Shangri-la."

"Well, you know how emotional Anna is. And you know how much we both love Rusty."

April fingered a button on the jacket draped across her knees. In spite of Noble's moderating words he didn't meet her gaze, but glanced about the room as if searching for a way out. It wasn't like Noble, and it worried April. "She told him she wished he could live with her. She seems to want to impress upon Rusty that her happiness is dependent upon him. That's a big burden to lay on anybody, Noble, much less a six-year-old. It isn't healthy, and it makes Rusty reluctant to spend time with his grandmother."

Noble's wandering eyes snapped back to April's face. "Are you saying you're going to keep Rusty away from us?"

She finally had his undivided attention. "I don't want to do that. Rusty loves you both and I want him to have a good relationship with you. But Anna has to stop clinging to him. Sometimes I wonder if she isn't a little mixed up and is confusing him with Paul. Why else would she talk to him about coming to live with her?"

Noble stiffened, and for a moment she wondered if she had gone too far. But when he spoke his tone was conciliatory. "She shouldn't have said that, and I think she knows it. But I'll talk to her about it, April. Just don't keep us from seeing Rusty. Anna's still grieving for Paul, but she's happy when Rusty is around." He sighed heavily. "It's about the only time she is."

April did not feel reassured by his last admission. Perhaps seeing this in her expression, Noble said hastily, "We had hoped to be able to have him Friday night. I could pick him up about five and bring him back Saturday afternoon."

"You'll speak to Anna before then?"

"Yes," he promised.

April agreed, partly because she didn't want Rusty to be estranged from his grandparents, and partly because she didn't wish to be in the position of opposing Noble on something that was important to him. Memories of the custody battle still haunted her. Noble did what he had to do to gain his ends.

Thursday she and Val worked late at the boutique, taking inventory. She arrived home at ten, hungry and very tired. Nan had already put Rusty to bed and was keeping a beef-and-potato casserole warm in the oven for April.

Smelling the food, April took off her coat and went straight to the kitchen. Nan was at the counter in her robe, rolling out pie dough.

"Why aren't you in bed with a good book?" April asked, opening the oven door. She reached for a potholder from a hook over the stove and lifted out the bubbly casserole.

Nan placed two circles of dough between layers of waxed paper. "I wasn't sleepy. Decided I might as well make pastry for next week's pies." She rolled the dough and waxed paper into a cylinder and placed them in the refrigerator.

"Hand me the milk, will you?" April said as she reached for a glass from the cabinet. After pouring the milk she sat down at the kitchen table and began to eat.

Nan wiped her hands on a red hand towel. "Did you finish your inventory?"

"Yes, we decided to stick it out until we were through. Thank goodness that's over for another year."

"Mr. Leyland was sorry to have missed you."

April's fork stopped halfway to her mouth. Her heart jerked. "Vic was here?"

"For about an hour. I assumed you'd forgotten that he

95

was coming. I offered to call you, but he wouldn't let me. Said he didn't want to interrupt your work, that he'd just chat with Rusty for a while."

"I didn't know he'd be here tonight." In fact, she had spent the past week making herself face up to the fact that Vic didn't want to see her again.

"He and Rusty played checkers, and I gave them milk and chocolate cake. At eight, when I reminded Rusty that it was his bedtime, Mr. Leyland said he'd be going, that he'd see you later. Should I have called you?"

"No, it's all right, Nan."

April looked at her plate, not wanting Nan to see the disappointment in her eyes. Nan watched her for a moment, then said, "I'm going to bed now. Good night."

"Good night, Nan."

April finished her meal, wondering if she should call Vic. Had he wanted to talk to her about something specific, perhaps take her to dinner? Maybe he'd just dropped in on the spur of the moment. And maybe it was best that they had missed each other. She wouldn't call him. Yet her disappointment at not being there when he came was so strong that Nan's succulent casserole suddenly had no more flavor than cardboard. She scraped the remains of her meal into the garbage disposal.

The next evening Rusty was with his grandparents and Nan went to a late movie with a friend. Alone in the apartment, April was alert to every tiny sound, half-anticipating a phone call or another visit from Vic. But neither the phone nor the doorbell rang all evening. She grew so restless that she finally called Elana to see if her friend wanted to come over, but Elana wasn't at home. At eleven April went to bed.

She lay in the darkness and listened to the wind whipping off the river and rattling the screen at her bedroom window. What was Vic doing at this moment? She tried to picture him asleep in his bedroom, but banished the image when she realized that a man like Vic Leyland most likely was not sleeping alone.

Sighing, she turned on her side and drew her knees up, clutching a pillow against her breast. At midnight she finally fell asleep.

The next day, determined to keep her mind occupied, she cleaned out her closet and Rusty's, folding no-longer-used clothing into plastic bags to give to the Salvation Army.

Noble brought Rusty home at six, refusing April's offer of coffee, saying he should get back to Anna. Rusty seemed unusually subdued and went straight to his bedroom. April followed him. He was sprawled on his back on the bed.

April sat down beside him and brushed a tangle of red hair off his forehead. "You feeling all right, honey?"

"I wanted to come home last night, but Grandpa wouldn't call you."

Wondering if he was coming down with something, April felt his forehead. Usually Rusty enjoyed his visits to his grandparents. "Did you feel sick?"

He looked up at her, his brown eyes clouded. "No. Grandma was crying and I thought maybe I was making her sad."

"Oh, honey, I'm sure it wasn't you." She stroked his cheek. "Maybe Grandma wasn't feeling well."

"She kept talking funny," Rusty said unhappily. He frowned. "Mom, does Vic want to be my daddy?"

Oh, God, what had Anna said to him? "Where did you get a notion like that?"

"Grandma kept asking me questions about Vic. She asked if Vic was going to marry you, and I said I didn't know. Is he, Mom?"

"Rusty, Vic and I don't know each other well enough to even be thinking about marriage."

"I'd like him to be my friend," Rusty said consideringly.

"I'm sure Vic would like that too."

He was silent for a moment and then suddenly he sat up and hugged April tightly. Against her breast, he muttered, "Grandma said it would make Daddy real sad if I ever got a new daddy."

Anger seared through April as she held her son close and murmured words of reassurance. What was wrong with Anna, to have said a thing like that to a child? Clearly she was trying to plant seeds of distrust of Vic in Rusty. If Noble had talked to Anna as he'd promised, it evidently hadn't done any good. Something had to be done to stop her saying such things to Rusty.

April worried about the situation through the rest of the weekend and at idle moments during the day Monday. By the time she left the boutique at five, she still hadn't decided how best to deal with Anna. She was beginning to fear that the woman was emotionally unstable. Never a strong woman, Anna had been near a breakdown when Paul died. And, instead of recovering from her grief with the passage of a year, she seemed to be unwilling to let it go. Refusing to let her see Rusty could do her irreparable harm. But April had to think of Rusty and what was best for him.

Deep in these troubling thoughts, April left the Forum. On the pavement in front of the mall she looked up and saw Vic hurrying across the street toward her. She didn't have time to think of what was best; she was aware only of how good it was to see him.

Smiling down at her, he took her arm. "Looks like I caught you just in time. Going home?"

She walked along with him, smiling foolishly. "Yes. I'm sorry we missed each other the other night."

"I should have phoned first. Rusty kept me company." She didn't reply as they made their way around a clump of people waiting at the bus stop. At the edge of the parking lot Vic halted and, since he was gripping her arm, April halted too. "I saw you when you came out of the Forum. You look troubled. Can I help?"

He stood there, looking so big and strong with his eyes reaching out to her. The wind barreled around the Forum and whistled past them. Already April's cheeks felt numb. For an instant she wanted to throw herself against him and feel his arms holding her, warming her, protecting her. "I am troubled, Vic, but I don't know what you can do."

He said decisively, "We'll go somewhere and talk about it. I wanted to ask you to have a drink with me anyway. I've been standing outside my building watching for you to come out for ten minutes."

Standing in the cold. Why should that make her feel so ridiculously pleased. "You have?"

He put his arm around her and they began walking back the way they had come. "We can go to Montague's in the Williams Plaza."

Nan would be expecting her, but she could phone home from the hotel. April hurried to keep up with Vic's long strides, her mind beginning to churn as the realization of what she was doing hit her. She was going with Vic willingly—eagerly—to a dark, intimate corner of the exclusive restaurant, Montague's. Because, from the moment she had seen him on the sidewalk, her good sense had deserted her and she had wanted to be alone with him.

CHAPTER SIX

Soft lighting glazed the fashionable restaurant in mellow gold, glistening the crystal and enclosing them in warmth. April and Vic were seated at a small corner table. The quiet drone of diners' voices accompanied by the tinkle of cutlery against glass bundled them in a cocoon of privacy.

As soon as they were seated Vic said, "Whatever the problem is, it can be solved. Don't look so forlorn."

Looking at his solid, confident bulk across the table, she thought, Yes, for you that must be true. You've probably never had a problem you couldn't solve.

She told him briefly that Anna's possessive attitude toward Rusty seemed to be getting worse, leaving out the hasty conclusion about Vic that Noble and Anna had jumped to.

The waiter came and asked if they'd like a cocktail. April shook her head. "I'll just have coffee."

"Why don't you have a brandy?" Vic said quietly. "It'll warm you."

She knew that he was right and also that she was keyed up enough without more caffeine. She nodded her ascent. "The last time Rusty spent the night with them," April said, bringing them back to Rusty and his grandparents, "it was so bad he wanted to come home before bedtime. Noble talked him out of it, but he was upset when he got home the next day."

101

The waiter appeared again with their drinks.

"I thought you were going to talk to Noble about his wife's behavior," Vic said.

"I did, but it hasn't helped."

"So what are you going to do about the situation?"

She sipped her brandy. "I don't know. I don't know if I'm unduly concerned, if maybe subconsciously I resent Noble and Anna."

"Because of the custody trial."

Surprised by the understanding in his words, she looked into his face. It was nearer her own than it had been a moment ago because he was leaning across the table toward her. "You mentioned the trial once before. How much do you know about it?"

"Only what I heard at the club, that Noble and Paul made you look incapable of raising your child alone."

She looked down at the brandy in her snifter. "I suppose you thought it must be true," she murmured. "The judge did."

"I didn't think about it one way or the other until I met you. Then I realized you'd been maligned."

She flashed him a grateful smile. "Oh, it wasn't anything as overt as that. Paul simply told the court that I had seen a psychiatrist a few times and had been given a prescription for tranquilizers. That was when I was trying to get up enough courage to leave Paul. I hadn't loved him for a long time. Sometimes I wonder if I ever did, but still . . ."

"Divorce, I don't care what the circumstances, makes you feel a certain amount of self-recrimination."

His gentle tone caused a warmth inside her, or perhaps it was the brandy. He went on. "Yet when Paul was given custody of Rusty, you went back to him. You must have

102

looked upon it as a second chance. Didn't you hope to salvage the marriage?"

"No, I knew that was impossible. But I didn't feel I had any other choice." A small ripple of unease ran through her and she pulled her cashmere sweater closer about her. It was one of those moments when she had a flash of unreasonable apprehension, a moment when she wondered if she'd dreamed Paul's death, if, when she went home, she would find him waiting there for her.

"I don't understand why you did it then. You weren't denied visiting rights in the custody case, were you?"

"No."

"Surely you could have had Rusty on the weekends. I know that wouldn't have been the ideal situation, but wasn't it a bit drastic to go back to Paul?"

Bleakness clouded her dark eyes. "Yes, it was drastic, but you didn't know Paul. He would have found a way to keep Rusty and me apart."

He found this difficult to accept. Surely no father would do that. But it was obvious that April believed Paul would have and, as she had said, he hadn't really known Paul.

"I was afraid to leave Rusty there alone with Paul." She was speaking softly, looking into her glass, talking as much to herself as to him.

What did she mean, afraid to leave Rusty alone with Paul? He was the boy's father after all.

"Near the end," she said after a moment, "I began to think about taking Rusty and running away. The night Paul was killed he'd gone to Oklahoma City and Rusty and I were alone in the house. I remember wishing that it could be like that all the time, just the two of us. Later that night the phone call came . . ."

Vic finished his brandy and turned the stem of the empty snifter back and forth between his fingers for a moment. Then his eyes returned to her face, keen with understanding. "And you blamed yourself, because of what you'd been thinking earlier."

How could this man whom she had met less than two months ago know so much about her? "I know it's irrational but, yes, I did. It was as if I'd wished him dead. Then, after the first shock of it, I was flooded with a feeling of being set free. I had twinges of guilt about that too. But for the first time I was glad I'd gone back to Paul. If I hadn't, Noble and Anna would probably have been given custody when Paul died. I half-expected Noble to try to take Rusty anyway. My friend Elana thought I was being paranoid. Maybe I was. As soon as I had the boutique to occupy my mind I began to get some perspective."

Clearly the custody trial had been devastating for her. Paul and Noble had hurt her terribly; maybe that's why she'd finally lost all faith in her husband. Vic wasn't sure that even yet she had come completely out from under the cloud of her unhappy marriage. He was sure only that his desire for her deepened every time they were together.

He thought of her too often when his mind should have concentrated on his work—the way she smelled, clean with the fresh lilac fragrance of the cologne she wore; the way her eyes sought his out when there were other people near, as if their eyes could communicate secrets that couldn't be said; the way she felt in his arms, fragile and womanly.

And then there was the wariness in her manner that made him want to protect her. There was something innocent in her, as if she were a dewy-eyed virgin and not a woman who had been married and borne a child, as if the ways of a man and a woman were mysteries to her. He wanted to take her home with him, to listen to the soft cadences of her voice, to follow the path of her thoughts and understand the deepest secrets of her mind, to lie with her and explore the loveliness of her body.

Lord, he had to stop thinking like that. Her mind was full of her problem with Rusty, not getting into bed with him. "From what you've told me, I think you have cause for concern. Forget about the Duboises and concentrate on what is best for Rusty. His grandmother shouldn't be allowed to see him if she upsets him."

The flash of fear in her eyes startled him. She said, "I know I'll have to stop Rusty's visits to them—somehow —if Anna keeps this up."

"April, are you afraid of Noble Dubois?"

She met his look unflinchingly. "Wouldn't you be? He helped take Rusty away from me once. Why wouldn't he do it again if I deny him and Anna permission to see Rusty?"

He was thoughtful for a moment before he said, "I've had enough dealings with Noble to know that he can be ruthless in business. But you're Rusty's only living parent. Even Noble Dubois can't change that."

"You weren't in that court, Vic! I never knew how easily people could take a few facts, twist them around, and make them mean something else entirely. After Paul and Noble got through, nobody would believe a word I said. When I went into that courtroom, I believed that no matter what Paul said the judge couldn't take Rusty away from his mother. I was so naive. I guess I didn't really know until then how much power the Duboises have. It . . . it was horrible."

He reached across the table and covered her shaking hand. "I'm sorry. I didn't understand what you'd been through, what they'd done to you. But you're too close to this thing to see it clearly. You've proved your ability to care for Rusty since Paul's death. If it came to it, the court would have to take that into consideration."

She wished that she could be as certain about her position as Vic seemed to be, but it made her feel better to talk to him. He was a compassionate, understanding man; she wouldn't have guessed that at their first two meetings. There were layers to Vic Leyland's personality; she found it intriguing to think about uncovering them one by one. It was this fascination more than gratitude that made her say yes when he asked to take her to dinner and a play at the Performing Arts Center the following evening.

She dressed with care for her date with Vic, choosing a black taffeta blouse with a sheer lace inset at the bodice and full sleeves. With the blouse she wore a swirling black velvet skirt and matching black velvet pumps. Her thick hair was brushed back away from her forehead without pins or combs, and it framed her face in a cascade of black waves, the ends falling in loose curls about her shoulders. As Vic helped her into her blue fox jacket the admiration in his eyes made whatever care she had taken seem worthwhile.

They went to Montague's again because it was just across the street from the Performing Arts Center. They had lobster and wine and by the time they had finished the long, leisurely meal, April was feeling relaxed and suffused with a sense of well-being.

She looked around the hotel supper club, taking in the understated elegance bathed in the romantic glow of the chandeliers. As Vic placed money and their check on the tiny silver tray left by the waiter, she admired the classically chiseled lines of his profile, the gleam of his dark hair in the soft light, the way his finely tailored navy, pinstriped jacket molded itself to his broad shoulders.

During dinner they had talked about many things, from their businesses to favorite vacation spots to how they had passed the summers as children.

Vic smiled at her. "Ready? The curtain goes up in ten minutes." He came around the table to help her from her chair.

She wanted to believe that her pounding heart and the weakness that invaded her limbs were caused by the wine. But the wine was only one contributing factor. Another, more powerful one was Vic's presence.

They settled into their seats only moments before the houselights were dimmed. It was a lighthearted musical comedy with brightly colored costumes and unashamedly sentimental songs.

Vic reached for her hand and enclosed it warmly in his. In the dimness she peered at their clasped hands resting on Vic's thigh, as if they belonged together. The light euphoria from the wine was still with her. She leaned her head against Vic's shoulder.

"Your hair smells good," he whispered, his breath warm against her forehead.

Laughter bubbled in her throat. She couldn't remember when she had felt so ridiculously happy. Was she drunk?

107

"Comfortable?" Vic inquired.

"Ummm."

Behind them somebody hissed, "Shhh!" April muffled a giggle against Vic's coat sleeve.

He angled a mock stern look down at her before he turned his attention to the stage. Or pretended to. Actually he was having considerable difficulty following what was going on behind the footlights. He was too aware of April's head resting on his shoulder. She stirred and her sweet-smelling hair brushed his cheek. The small hand clasped under his seemed to be burning a hole through his trousers into his thigh. He smothered a groan. She didn't know what she was doing to him. At intermission he'd go outside and walk up and down in front of the theater for a few minutes.

As the play progressed April got caught up in the romantic story. Her contented drowsiness left her, and soon she was sitting up straight, engrossed in the humorous tale of two lovers who overcame every obstacle to be together. At intermission Vic said he needed to stretch his legs and went outside. He returned just as the play resumed, so there was no chance for conversation until they were leaving the theater.

"Did you like it?" Vic asked. He took her arm to steer her through the crowd and out onto the sidewalk.

She turned the collar of her fox jacket up around her face to ward off the February cold. "Yes. I can't remember when I've laughed so much."

He had enjoyed hearing her laugh—almost more than the play. Lightheartedness was a facet that he hadn't seen in her before.

"I loved the songs," she went on. "It was nice to spend

108

a couple of hours in a world where everything turns out perfectly in the end."

They had reached Vic's Cadillac. When he had the engine going and the heater on, he said, "Speaking of endings, I don't want our evening to end just yet."

"It's ten o'clock," April said.

He headed the car toward the freeway. "Early yet. Let's go to my place for a nightcap before I take you home."

She tilted her head to look over at him. It had been a wonderful evening, and she was as reluctant as Vic to have it end. Also, she admitted to some curiosity about the place where Vic lived. Once he'd said something about a ranch. "Where do you live?"

"A town house near Sixty-first and Memorial. We can be there in ten minutes."

Ten minutes. A quick nightcap. And then home. "All right," she said. "But I can't stay long."

Vic's town house sat on a hill overlooking the city. The living room reminded her of Vic—handsome, clean, and comfortable. The carpet and two couches covered with a coarse, nubby fabric were a soft pearl gray. Floor-to-ceiling shelves on the wall behind one of the couches were crammed with an extensive collection of books. More visual interest was supplied by a rich burgundy leather ottoman, a rectangular coffee table made from shiny Mexican marble, and plump burgundy and green throw pillows. Logs, kindling, and rolled newspapers had been laid in the limestone-faced fireplace. Vic removed the brass screen and bent to light the fire.

April stood at the expansive bank of windows while Vic got the fire going, then went after their drinks. Spread below her the city was an array of jewels strewn from the river to the suburbs on the south, east, and north.

When Vic came back into the room with a glass of red wine for her and a beer for himself, she turned and said, "This view is a marvel!"

"Isn't it? It's the main reason I bought this particular house." He handed her the wineglass.

After arranging a couple of throw pillows, she settled comfortably in a corner of the couch that faced the fireplace. Vic sat beside her and they watched the fire and sipped their drinks in companionable silence for a moment. She gazed at Vic's profile over the rim of her glass. He had removed his jacket and tie, and his long legs in the pinstriped trousers were stretched out in front of him. Firelight played over his jaw, the angle of his cheekbone, the thick strands of his dark hair. His eyes were narrowed, pensive, as he gazed into the fire. Slowly he set his glass on the marble coffee table and turned to look at her.

She finished her wine and set the glass aside, feeling suddenly shy. She rubbed her hands along her sleeves.

"Cold?"

Not when his eyes burned over her like that. She glanced away. "Not really."

"The fire will have it plenty warm in here in no time, but I can turn up the heat if you like."

"No, that isn't necessary. I—I guess I should be going home."

"You don't really want to leave yet," he murmured with husky certainty, and bent his head toward her. His warm breath ruffled a wisp of hair at her temple.

Her head jerked up. "How—how do you know what I want?"

He examined her face, scrutinizing her features as if he

meant to sketch them. Yet there was more than mere admiration in his look. He wanted to delve into her mind. It frightened her.

"I know," he said.

Her lips parted, and he laid his forefinger against them. "Please don't, April," he said quietly. "Don't fight your feelings tonight. Nothing will happen that you don't want."

Sighing, for he was right when he said she didn't want to go yet, she sat mutely as he ran his hands up her arms and cupped the back of her head. "I've wanted to get you alone like this for weeks," he said, smiling down at her. "I think about you all the time."

Well, she thought about him, too, but she wasn't idiot enough to say so.

"There's no one here to interrupt us, and I unplugged the telephone." His head lowered over hers and he kissed her lips, a soft, searching kiss that sought only to soothe and demanded nothing. But when he raised his head, she was breathless with its effect.

His fingers slid through her hair. "Your hair is beautiful," he whispered. "I like it best when you wear it down like this." He caressed her cheek with his lips, then returned to her mouth, moving his lips against hers in a sweet savoring that made her mouth open involuntarily before she was aware of it.

Lifting his head, he sought her eyes and held them. For bright spinning moments he hesitated, as if giving her time to change her mind, his breath warm against her skin. She was aching with anticipation by the time his tongue glided over her lips, then slipped between them, coaxing her mouth to accept its gentle penetration.

His hand moved languorously down her spine to the

small of her back, where it lay heavy and warm for several moments before it returned to her nape and began slowly to unzip the back opening of her blouse.

Her head reeling, she was only vaguely aware when he pulled the blouse down off her shoulders and freed her breasts from the confinement of her black lace bra.

He lifted his head and her breath came out in a raspy, whispery sigh. "Vic . . ." His unwavering eyes held hers, and she felt drugged, her senses dazed by the intensity of the passion she read in the depths of his dilated pupils.

Her hands moved between them and, to her own swirling confusion, her shaking fingers found the buttons of his shirt and managed to loose them while she became drunk on the feel of his lips nuzzling her cheek, the masculine scent of his skin, the gentle way his hand slid down to cup the underswell of one breast. She closed her eyes and her breath caught in her throat. "Your skin is like satin, April. Your breast fills my hand as if it were made for this."

Her palms splayed against the roughness of the dark hair covering his chest, and her breath released itself in a soft moan.

The fire bathed them in its golden warmth; the light-dotted velvet blackness outside pressed against the windows, enclosing them. The minutes drifted by in a haze of euphoria. And April sat spellbound as Vic made slow, rapturous love to her.

His mouth, soft and warm and moist, toyed gently with her lips, her nape, the small, sensitive curves of her ear. One hand buried itself in her hair while the other caressed the swell of her breasts and gently rotated the turgid crests. Her head fell back against the cushions of

112

the couch, her black lashes lowered to rest against the translucent ivory of her cheeks.

Deep inside her she felt a sweet, fierce tugging, a sensuous arousal that she had never experienced with her husband, even in the early days of their marriage. Paul had cursed her, called her "the ice maiden," because she couldn't respond to his aggressive, sometimes painful, lovemaking. Now it felt as if that buried intimate, feminine core of her was thawing and stirring with a tingling life of its own.

She had never been kissed like this. Vic was lingering, taking his time, as if he could go on kissing her and touching her all night.

He dipped his head, and his tongue gently stroked her hardened nipple. She gasped at the pleasure generated by his mouth and tongue as he sucked and caressed that exquisitely sensitive part of her.

"Oh, Vic . . . yes . . . please."

"I want you," he said in a voice husky with passion. His hand lifted her skirt and slid beneath to cup her.

In one instant, as his fingers rubbed against that most intimate core of her, all the warm, tingling pleasure drained out of her and was replaced by unreasoning fear. Her eyes flew open and she stiffened.

For a moment she had lost her bearings; she had thought that it was Paul holding her and what had been a sweet giving and taking of sensual pleasure suddenly seemed a demanding invasion. Looking into passion-glazed eyes, she saw that it was Vic, not Paul. Paul was dead. He could never hurt her again.

But the mood had been shattered. Muscles that had been drowsily relaxed were tense and quivering. She stared at Vic. "Please, stop . . . stop touching me."

113

Her dark eyes were huge, pain-filled. Somehow Vic managed to get a rein on his passion, which had built to near-explosive proportions, and he let her go. What had he done wrong? She sat up, tugging her skirt down and pulling her blouse up to cover her breasts.

"Did I hurt you?"

She gave one quick shake of her head, refusing to look at him, and the firelight caught the tumble of black waves and shimmered in blue-black highlights. She clutched a throw pillow on her knees, her fingers plucking agitatedly at the cord trim.

Vic watched her, pondering with puzzled brows what she was thinking. He wanted to touch her, but he didn't dare. Her rigid posture warned him off.

Crumpling the pillow, she brought it up until half her face was hidden from him. She spoke to him from behind the pillow. "No, not you . . . never you. It's me. There's something wrong with me."

He pulled the pillow away from her face, tossing it to the floor. She turned her face aside and refused to open her eyes. God, he wished she wouldn't look like that, so wounded and vulnerable. He had to touch her; it seemed the only sensible thing to do. Very gently he smoothed her hair back from her face. "What are you talking about? You're the most nearly perfect woman I've ever known."

"Oh, God . . ." She propped her elbows on her knees and covered her face with her hands. Her muffled voice was thick with unshed tears. "You don't understand. I'm not like other women. He told me he needed me, and I tried to be what he wanted. But I couldn't . . . I couldn't . . ."

Vic hardly knew what to do or say next. He'd said the

same thing to her, that he needed her. Her hair was a silken tumble of shimmering black around her face. "Are you trying to tell me you're frigid?" he asked quietly.

She nodded, her face still hidden in her hands.

He touched her shoulder. She was trembling. "April, look at me."

"Don't touch me."

His palm closed firmly about the curve of her shoulder. For a long moment she didn't move. Then slowly she lifted her head and met his look. His fingers brushed the tears from her cheeks. "You need to be touched, love," he said with exquisite tenderness.

April's breath caught on a sob as his hand slipped to the back of her neck. "Vic, don't feel sorry for me . . . please. I don't want that from you."

"Shh, love," he whispered, and leaned closer to kiss her forehead. "April, did Paul tell you that you were frigid?"

"Yes," she murmured, "but he didn't have to tell me."

"Honey, he was a liar. A little while ago you were taking pleasure from our lovemaking. You were all soft and eager in my arms. It was the normal, natural response of a woman to a man."

She looked away from him, pondering this. She had found delights with Vic that she'd never known with Paul, as long as he was only kissing and caressing her. But when he had moved toward the natural consequence of their actions, she had frozen. The pain Paul had inflicted on her had suddenly filled her mind, as if it were more than a dark memory, as if it were happening again.

But Vic was so different from Paul. He touched her heart and her soul. She wanted him to understand. She wanted . . . what? To be what he deserved, to pour herself out for him. She was falling in love with Vic. . . . *Oh, dear God!*

"He killed something in me, Vic. It's gone. I couldn't respond to my husband even though I tried so hard." There. She had been as honest with him as she could be. Surely he would realize now that she was a hopeless case. The thought of never seeing him again was a sharp pain in her chest. But he had a right to know the truth. She got up abruptly and went to stand at the window, her back to Vic. She felt ashamed, a pitiful excuse for a woman.

Reflected in the glass, she saw Vic stand, run his hands through his hair, and come to stand behind her. He straightened her blouse and closed the zipper, then let his hands come to rest on her shoulders. "Didn't it ever occur to you that it might have been Paul's fault, not yours?"

She looked down, pressing her forehead against the cold glass. Had he guessed the dark secret of her marriage? Oh, God, she couldn't talk to him about *that.* He would lose whatever respect he had for her, if any remained after the way she had behaved just now.

"A sensitive woman needs to be wooed gently, cherished, loved." His warm breath in her hair, his gentle hands resting in the crux of her shoulders and neck made her feel weak.

"Paul didn't know the meaning of gentleness or love. He was cruel . . . abusive . . ." She clamped her mouth shut, appalled at how much she had revealed.

Vic's hands, which had been massaging the tense muscles at the base of her neck, went very still. She had never meant to say so much. She lost all sense, all inhibition, when she was with Vic. Dear Lord, she was already deeply in love with him. What an idiot she was! The hopelessness of her situation welled up in her and she couldn't hold back the tears that spilled silently down her cheeks.

"He hurt you?" His tone was a tense mixture of incredulity and fury. He turned her around, grasped her chin in his hand, and tilted it up so that she had to look at him. "Answer me, April. Did he abuse you?"

His fingers tightened on her chin and she winced. On a sob she whispered, "Yes, please . . . you're hurting me."

He flung his hand away and stared at it for an instant as if it belonged to somebody else. Then with a muttered oath he gathered her into his arms and drew her against him. "I'm sorry. . . . Oh, April, if I'd known . . ."

She was crying uncontrollably now, her face turned into the healing of Vic's shoulder, her tears wetting his shirt. She wept as she hadn't wept in years. Her body shook with the anguish that she had held inside far too long. Her racking sobs went on and on.

"It's all right, April," he crooned, his voice thick with emotion, holding her, kissing her ear, the side of her neck and finally, when she lifted her head, the wet skin of her closed eyelids and cheeks. "It's all right, love."

CHAPTER SEVEN

They got out of the Cadillac and, heads bent against the fierce wind, ran hand in hand to April's apartment building. Inside, Vic put his arm around her as they walked along the dimly lighted hallway to her door.

She felt limp and exhausted after her siege of weeping. Vic had been incredibly patient, holding her and murmuring comforts until she could compose herself.

She shivered as she searched through her clutch purse for her key. They had talked little during the drive and, self-conscious about the continued silence, April said the first thing that came to mind. "Brrr. I hate wintertime." She found the key and inserted it in the door. But when she opened it and reached to turn the knob, Vic's hand closed over hers and stopped her.

"The weather's perfect in St. Thomas now," he said, looking down at her with a new tenderness. He understood how exposed she was feeling. "People are sailing or swimming or strolling barefoot on the beach. Have you ever been to the Virgin Islands?"

"No," she said, trying to sound lighthearted, to erase the worry lurking beneath the tenderness in Vic's eyes. "And I think it's mean of you to talk about it when the weather's so dreadful here."

His finger lightly traced the arch of her brow. She was suddenly conscious of how awful she must look, her makeup gone, her eyes swollen from weeping. Vic said,

"I'm thinking of going there next weekend . . . if you'll come with me."

She blinked surprised eyes at him. "Just the two of us?"

"Uh-huh," he murmured. "We could both use some time off. It might even do you good to be away from Rusty for a couple of days."

"Oh, Vic. You're kind to ask, but it wouldn't be fair to you."

Sympathy tightened in his chest like a heavy spring. He pulled April against his body until she was inside the circle of his arms. He rested his chin on the top of her head. "I want you to come with me."

"It would only be embarrassing for us both," she whispered. "I'd disappoint you."

Spreading his feet wide for balance, he rocked her back and forth gently, as he might have comforted a child. "You could never do that, April. You've been hurt and you've taken refuge inside your shell. But you're a woman, capable of all the feelings any other woman is capable of."

"You don't know . . ." she murmured unhappily.

Did he dare tell her that he was falling in love with her? No. Not now, after what had happened between them. She would think he'd said that because he felt sorry for her or, worse yet, that it was a bribe to get her to go to St. Thomas with him. Hatred for Paul Dubois burned in his gut; Dubois had taken her fragile innocence and smashed it. This woman, who trembled in his arms, had suffered unspeakable things at the hands of her husband and had gone on suffering for the sake of her child. It was a wonder she could stay in the same room with a man. He knew that he had to handle her with infinite care. First he must teach her to trust him before he could risk baring his soul to her.

His arms tightened around her, as if to shield her from further hurt. "I don't have any expectations, sweetheart," he said. He moved one hand over her jacket, feeling the defeated slump of her back beneath the fur. "No motive in asking you to go except that I want to be with you. We'll have separate bedrooms. You can trust me not to make demands. I have no right to ask anything of you that you don't want to give. I'm sorry about what happened earlier. I was a fool. I should have known. . . ."

April pressed her face into the warm, dark haven of his neck, seeking comfort. She had never known that any man could be so caring, so tender. "It wasn't your fault."

Her unwillingness to blame him made Vic feel shame. With his blundering assumptions he had reduced her to tears and this trembling, desperate need for comfort. Somehow he would make it up to her. His head bent low, he kissed her brow.

"Will you think about going to St. Thomas?"

She lifted her face so that his lips brushed her cheek, and the contact was like a healing balm. She wanted to accept. She wanted to stop being afraid and trust Vic. "Yes, I'll think about it."

"I'll call you tomorrow night." He was desperate to have her with him, at any cost. "I meant what I said, April. We'll enjoy the days together and sleep apart. You'll never have to be afraid of me. Never."

His words didn't bring the comfort to her that Vic intended. A small frisson of unhappiness flowed through her. What she wanted, she realized with a shock, was not a platonic friendship with Vic. What she wanted was for him to lead her farther along the path of her womanhood

121

where they had ventured earlier that evening. She wanted to be free to feel and experience things that other women knew. If anyone could set her free, she knew it would be Vic. But could Vic perform that great a miracle?

Slowly she lifted her face until her lips touched his. The kiss was a soft caress of reassurance on Vic's part, a tender plea for understanding on April's.

He reached out and opened the door for her. "We'll talk tomorrow," he said huskily as she slipped inside.

In the darkness April leaned against the closed door. She knew what her answer would be when Vic called tomorrow night. She would go with him; but that was as far as her thoughts could take her. She didn't know what would happen in St. Thomas; perhaps it was better that she didn't know. But she knew that they had reached a point in their relationship where she would have to risk something, or it would end.

At least, she thought as she found her way to her bedroom, he knew the worst about her and he hadn't been revolted.

They arrived at their hotel in Charlotte Amalie late Friday night. As soon as the bellboy had shown them to their separate rooms, Vic came in through a connecting door and found April standing on the balcony overlooking the harbor. The tangy smell of the sea wafted on the gentle breeze. Lights in the buildings lining the harbor across the bay glittered like distant gems. April had shed her jacket and shoes and stood with her hands resting on the railing, the faint wind tangling in her dark hair.

She heard him and looked over her shoulder with a smile. Her beautiful face was touched softly by the lamplight from the bedroom. "Oh, Vic, it's lovely!"

Standing behind her, he enclosed her in his arms, pulling her back against him. "Wait till you see it in the sunlight," he murmured. "We're getting up early, by the way. I have a full day planned tomorrow. First, we'll—"

"Don't tell me," she interrupted. "I want to be surprised."

They were silent for several minutes. April leaned back in his arms, her arms shielding her breasts, treasuring the solid feel of his body against her back. She gazed down at the lights reflecting on the dark mirror of the harbor and wondered what would happen when they went inside.

But Vic had learned not to pressure her. He was wiser now and, even while he contemplated going in to his lonely bed momentarily, he felt an elation he hadn't known in years.

She stroked the hair on the back of his hand. She relaxed and let her slender weight lean against his greater strength. She felt dazed with tiredness after their journey.

Trying to stifle a yawn, she said, "What time will we have breakfast?"

"Eight, I thought. I'll ring you at seven. Okay?"

"Ummm."

He bent his head down until his cheek brushed hers. The day's growth of beard abraded her skin lightly. For some reason, it made her smile. "I'd better let you go to bed now." Reluctantly he released her from his arms.

She turned and his hand came up to cup her chin. "Sweet dreams," he said huskily. With a careful poignancy his lips fastened to hers and he pulled her against him until her breasts were pressed tightly to his chest. Slowly April slipped her arms about his waist.

"Good night," he said when he finally lifted his head.

She smiled wistfully. " 'Night."

She watched him walk across her bedroom and step into his, closing the connecting door behind him. He was keeping his promise, but she realized that she felt bereft now that a wall separated them. On a sigh of mingled disappointment and gratitude, she went in to get ready for bed. She wished that she could have called him back. If only he had said he loved her.

Over lunch the next day in the hotel's terrace restaurant, April said, "Well, what's on the agenda for this afternoon?" She had slipped her tired feet out of her sandals and curled her bare toes against the warm flagstone paving. They had spent the morning strolling along the main street, browsing in one shop after another.

"I want to buy you something," Vic had insisted as April shook her head over table linens and china and jewelry of every description.

"Why should you buy me anything?" she asked finally.

"I want you to have something that will make you remember this weekend every time you look at it."

Glancing up into his craggily handsome face, she had felt her heart turn over. As if she could ever forget this weekend! Finally she had chosen a water color of the harbor from a local artist's display on the sidewalk outside the historic Grand Hotel.

Now Vic said, "We could stay here and swim in the hotel pool. Or we could take the ferry to St. John and go snorkeling at Trunk Bay."

April's gaze lingered on the blue sea and sky that were so nearly the same color that it was difficult to find the horizon, then admired two white cruise ships docked at the harbor. Squinting against the light, she scanned the dazzlingly white sand beach that began just beyond the terrace and was already crowded with sunbathers. A beautiful hedge of yellow-flowering green shrubs bordered the terrace—the ginger flower, Vic had told her, state flower of the U.S. Virgin Islands. At the moment she felt as though she could sit on the terrace for the rest of the afternoon. Everywhere she turned, the view was breathtaking. Unbelievable to think that back home in Tulsa the temperature was in the thirties and a knife-sharp wind was blowing out of the north.

She turned back to Vic. "I wouldn't want to miss St. John."

His smile was approving. "Good. The next ferry leaves at two. Can you be ready in twenty minutes?"

She assured him that she could. In her room she put on a red maillot with a plunging neckline and a short white terry cover-up. A few minutes later Vic came to get her, wearing navy swim trunks and a pale blue knit shirt.

Arriving at St. John's Cruz Bay harbor, they climbed aboard a shuttle going to Trunk Bay. The snorkeling trail in the blue water of the bay was clearly marked. They spent an hour following it, equipped with rented snorkel masks and flippers, then spread towels on the white sand for sunbathing.

April stretched out on her stomach and Vic sat down beside her, his knees drawn up. "Where's the suntan lotion?"

She produced it from her canvas bag. He poured lotion between her shoulder blades and began to rub it slowly over her back.

She rested her head on her folded arms. "How often do you come here?" she asked drowsily.

His hand smoothed lotion down the length of her spine to the small of her back where her maillot began. The

125

slow, massaging movements made her want to stretch like a lazy cat. "A couple of times a year. I spent the Christmas holiday here year before last."

Quickly he smoothed lotion on the back of her legs, as if he were in a hurry to be finished. She wondered if he had come there alone in the past, or with another woman. It didn't bear thinking about for long. She was sorry when he stopped touching her and began to apply the lotion to his legs and chest. His big body was becoming familiar to her now. She enjoyed watching him covertly as his hand ran over the muscles of his chest and flat stomach. She admired the way the muscles of his thighs tensed when he bent his legs, how the sun glinted streaks in his dark hair.

He capped the lotion bottle, laid it aside, and stretched out on his side, facing her, his head supported on the heel of his hand. "I thought everybody spent Christmas with their family," she said inanely.

He was so close to her that his breath fell tantalizingly on the side of her face. He reached out to twine a black curl around his finger. "My parents have lived in Australia for the past five years. Dad sold everything he had and bought a small sheep station there. It's been a dream of his for years. God knows why. He raised me and my younger sisters on a farm in Nebraska. It was a continual battle with bugs and the weather just to put enough food on the table for the five of us. I couldn't wait to get away from there. Nor could my sisters. They both married at eighteen and moved away. I was in grad school by then. We're not a very close family."

"I'm sorry . . ." she murmured, not knowing why she said it, except that he had sounded unhappy as he was telling her about his family.

He frowned, threading his fingers through her hair, smoothing it back off her face. "Why?"

"You sounded regretful."

He flipped on his back and closed his eyes. "Sometimes I feel guilty for deserting them. I went away to college at eighteen, and I never went back except for a few days once a year. I had to work my way through, so I didn't have much time for going home. But I didn't really want to go. Dad had expected me to stay and take over the farm. I told him I'd rather dig ditches. He never completely forgave me."

"Did your mother feel the same way?"

"It's hard to tell with Mom. She doesn't say much, and she's never disagreed openly with Dad in her life. She just looks at you with a sorrowful expression as if she's thinking, 'Now, why do you want to cause trouble in the family?' She does write me now and then."

"And your sisters?"

He shrugged, his eyes still closed. "The last time I visited them, three years ago, I realized that we had absolutely nothing in common and we didn't feel at ease with each other. I think they resent me for getting an education and being successful in business. Their husbands work at manual labor—the money isn't great."

She watched the rise and fall of his chest. "But they could have had an education if they'd been willing to work for it, like you."

"I guess it didn't seem so to them at the time." He threw his arm across his forehead to shade his eyes and looked over at her. "I've tried to make up for some of it by sending Mom and Dad a monthly check. But sometimes I wonder if they think I'm trying to buy back their approval." He laughed unhappily. "Hell, maybe they're right. Maybe every time we bring in another well, I'm really thinking, 'Hey, Dad. Hey, Mom, look at me. See how successful your boy is.'"

Without thinking, April pulled a clean tissue from her canvas bag and blotted the perspiration on Vic's upper lip. She sensed that he had told her things that he'd never talked to anyone about before. For the first time, she saw that there was much more to Vic than the confident, successful, surface man. There was a lonely, vulnerable core inside. She wished that she were capable of comforting him. "You're too hard on yourself."

Vic sought her eyes and held them for so long that her throat felt too tight for her to breathe. She thought he would kiss her.

Instead, he said quietly, "I think I miss being close to my nieces and nephews more than anything. I send them gifts for birthdays and Christmas, but it isn't the same as having a relationship with them. Maybe when they're older I can invite them out here during their summer vacations. But that's enough about me. Tell me about your family."

"I'm an only child. My father died when I was ten, and my mother when I was in college. There was insurance, so I was able to finish and get my degree. I planned to work in advertising, but then I married Paul, and he wanted me to stay at home."

She put her head down and shielded her eyes from him with her hand as she spoke unemotionally, with little inflection, as if she were reading from a prepared script. Yet Vic felt that he could detect her broken dreams between the lines. In trying to be brave, she cut straight into his heart. He wanted to hold her so badly that it took a superhuman effort merely to grasp the hand with which she was shielding herself from him and lower it to the towel between them. "I'm sorry I asked," he said gently. "This is now, and I don't want it spoiled for either of us by unhappy memories."

Lacing her fingers through his, she brought their hands to her cheek. "Let's not think about the past or home while we're here." She determined not even to mention Rusty for the next twenty-four hours. She had left him in Nan's care, and she knew he was all right. For one day, she wanted to pretend that there was no past, no future, no place but these warm emerald islands in a sapphire sea.

They idled away another hour and a half before returning to St. Thomas. It was six o'clock when they got back to their hotel. Vic followed her into her room and stretched out on her bed, his hands behind his head. "What would you like to do this evening?"

"Right now, all I want is a shower and a nap," April told him, heading for the bathroom.

She expected Vic to be gone when she returned. But he still lay on her bed, sound asleep. He'd pulled the sheet up to his chest against the chill of the air-conditioning. She walked closer to the bed and saw his damp bathing trunks and knit shirt in a heap on the floor. Her pulse leaped as she realized he was sleeping in the raw—in her bed.

She stood over him for a long moment, chewing the inside of her cheek. She could go into Vic's room for her nap. But she didn't want to do that. What she really wanted to do was to lie beside Vic and fall asleep, knowing that she could touch him merely by moving her hand fractionally. Well, why not? He was dead to the world.

She went to the balcony doors and drew the draperies

closed, throwing the room into soft gray shadows. She returned to the bed, hesitating for just an instant. She was wearing a short terry robe over her panties and bra, and she left the robe on as she lowered herself carefully to the bed, stretching out on top of the covers. She turned on her side so that she could watch Vic sleep. His lashes lay on the taut, tanned skin of his cheekbones like half-moon smudges of black paint. There was a faint hump at the bridge of his nose that she'd barely noticed before; it looked as if the nose had been broken and poorly set, if set at all. But instead of detracting from his appearance, it added a rakish, masculine touch that was very appealing. His dark-haired chest rose and fell softly above the border of the white sheet. There were a few grains of sand on the shoulder next to her and, before April was conscious of it, her hand reached out to brush the sand away. Frowning, she clenched her hand into a fist just before the contact was made and lowered it to her side. Vic's body warmth, the clean smell of his skin, his deep, even breathing, filled her senses. A contented smile touched her lips as she edged closer to him, drew up her knees, and closed her eyes.

Later she awoke, her body pliant with drowsy lassitude. Stretching, she opened her eyes. The room was in deep shadow. Then she remembered that Vic had been sleeping beside her. She turned her head. His head rested on his bent arm, and he was looking at her with a mesmeric intensity.

She was shaken. His breathtaking nearness, his nakedness beneath the sheet, the way his eyes were riveted to her face, washed over her and left her weak. How long had he been watching her?

She lowered her lashes to hide her eyes from him. Vic

continued to watch her face, and his hand came up to curve warmly about the back of her neck.

"Hi." His voice was sensually hoarse with sleep.

Where had her breath gone? "Hi . . . we must have slept for a long time . . . it's getting dark . . . we should get ready for dinner. . . ."

He drew her next to him, with his hand at her nape, until her head rested on his shoulder. "The natives here have a saying," he murmured into her hair. " 'Too much hurry, get dere tomorra, tek time, get dere today.' "

He imitated the musical patois of the natives' English perfectly. She smiled. "I suppose you were trifling with a beautiful native girl when she told you that."

He chuckled and tugged the sheet from beneath her, covering them both with it. Her arm rested on his hard chest. She snuggled against him, delighting in the feel of springy curls and the deep, even beat of his heart beneath her palm.

"Maybe," he said, a smile in his voice. "Are you jealous?"

She turned her face up to look at him and said bluntly, "Yes."

He smiled down at her. "Good."

Playfully she tugged at a chest hair. "What do you mean, good?"

He jerked and grabbed her hand, growling, "If you're jealous, it means you have feelings for me." Their smiles died as his unwavering eyes held hers. His head lowered and he kissed her . . . a soft, searching kiss.

Her dazed senses responded to the intensity of the passion she felt in him. Her lips softened and parted in welcome as his fingers loosed the tie of her robe and released the clasp of her bra. He caressed the rise of her breasts

131

and moved lower to discover the turgid nipples. Her breathing seemed to stop.

The minutes stretched out like spun sugar. April's head lolled back against the pillow and her arms found their way around Vic's neck, her fingers delving into his hair and caressing the corded muscles in the back of his neck and the hard planes of his back. She lay enchanted as Vic's hands and mouth slowly explored her body, and his rapturous spell wrapped itself around her.

As her breath sounded in a raspy, whispering sigh she murmured, "Vic . . . oh, Vic . . . I don't know what's happening."

His mouth played gently with her ear's shell-like rim. "Don't think about it," he whispered. "Forget everything except that I'm a man and you're a woman and we have all night to spend together." He kissed the side of her neck, her lashes, returning at last to lay claim to her trembling lips. His tongue dipped boldly into her mouth again and again, an erotic reminder of that deeper, more intimate contact.

Once more she felt that fierce tugging within her, the sweet excitement that she had experienced only once before, that night in Vic's town house. Her body arched against him and, as he lowered his head, she didn't even recognize her own voice as she pleaded, "Yes, Vic . . . kiss me there."

Swiftly he finished removing her robe and bra, then tugged off her panties. He pulled the sheet back. "I want to see you, love," he said in a voice hoarse with desire. His eyes raked the pale, gleaming contours of her body. "So beautiful." He lowered his head to the dark, thrusting crest of one breast, enclosing it sweetly in the moist heat of his mouth. His tongue gently laved the aching nipple.

April lost all sense of time or place. It was as if the boundaries of her self had melted away, and there was nothing but feeling. The throbbing within her deepened as Vic's mouth claimed her lips, her nipples, her stomach, tracking her body with his moist kisses as the tropic night enclosed them and the verdant earth seemed to hold its breath, waiting. . . .

His hand cupped the gentle mound of her womanhood, his fingers—with exquisite slowness—finding that secret, feminine core of her. Hardly aware of what she was doing, she arched her hips in a silent plea for a release that she sensed but had never experienced.

"Vic," she whispered, the word only barely coherent.

His hand moved with an increased tempo as her body writhed and arched, seeking she knew not what.

And then she knew.

Suddenly a wave of rapturous sensation burst in her loins, its ripples spreading throughout her body and leaving her spent and shaken. Only after it was over did she realize that tears had wet her cheeks. Never had she experienced anything like this before.

Vic held her until the tremors left her body, and she was limp in his arms. Then he bent over her and brushed the tears from her cheeks. "Don't cry, April. It's all right."

Dazed, she smiled at him. How tenderly he had aroused her, slowly bringing to life that long-dead, essential feminine essence that she had believed lacking in herself. But he had shown her, with such sweet assurance, that she was a whole woman. And he had given no thought to his own assuagement, only hers. "No, it isn't.

Not yet. I want to give you as much pleasure as you've given me."

"Honey, you don't have to. . . ."

Vic was so aroused that he couldn't continue to look at her kiss-swollen lips and the glowing satiation in her eyes for fear of falling on her and losing all control. He lay rigid, looking at the ceiling.

She turned on her side, cupped his face in her hands and pulled it down to hers. She kissed him with a soft lingering of gratitude and overflowing love. "I do want to."

Needing no further encouragement, his built-up tension was released in a deep groan as he moved over her. April treasured the weight of his body. She wrapped her arms around him and with a soft whimper of happiness took him into herself.

CHAPTER EIGHT

She lay cradled in Vic's arms, feeling protected and so happy that she was afraid to close her eyes and give in to her drowsiness, for fear she would wake up and find it had all been a dream.

She had given Vic as much as he had given her; giddy with thankfulness because she had been able to do that, she pressed a kiss into the damp crook of his neck.

His arms tightened around her. "April . . ." His voice was thick with emotion. "I didn't bring you here for this. Please, believe me."

"I do believe you. It just happened."

"You aren't sorry?"

With sudden shyness she hid her face against his shoulder. When she spoke her words were muffled against his warm, damp skin. "How can I be sorry when you've made me feel like a woman again?"

His large hand cradled the back of her head. "You are a beautiful, wonderful woman. I love you, April."

The words hung suspended in the air for a moment as April tried to convince herself that she had really heard them. Then she hugged them to herself and, leaning back against the pillow, she looked into his face.

His eyes were deep and mysterious in the shadows. "I love you desperately," he said.

"I love you too." She wished that she could compose a

song or a poem to expand upon those four simple words. Somehow they didn't seem enough.

He leaned over her and fastened his mouth to hers. It felt so natural, so right that a voice said in her head, *There will never be another man in all the world for me.*

Opening herself, she let her tongue touch his teeth, inviting him to explore anew the recesses of her mouth. His hand closed about her breast, and she covered his hand with hers and pressed it to her.

He moaned, and she grew bolder. Her tongue darted hungrily. Never had she felt so open to anyone before, so much a woman.

After several moments he drew back and shook his head and muttered, "If we don't stop this, we'll never get to dinner."

She didn't feel rebuffed, as she would have only a few hours ago. She understood that he wanted her, but he could postpone that particular pleasure while they went somewhere to eat and laugh and look into each other's eyes. That would even heighten the pleasure they would take in each other later.

She slid from the bed, smiling down at him. "Now that you mention it, I'm starved. Where are we going?"

His gaze raked her small, firm ivory breasts and the delectable curve of her hips. "Alfredo's in Frenchtown."

She turned and padded toward the bathroom, moving with the natural grace of a child. She was so incredibly beautiful that it made his throat ache. He cleared his throat.

"April."

She turned as she reached the bathroom door. "Yes?"

"Marry me."

He sensed rather than saw her sudden tenseness. He

136

sat up and let his legs slide off the side of the bed and kept on looking at her.

"I don't want to talk about that, Vic," she said in a taut voice, one she might have used to a casual acquaintance who has asked a too personal question.

Her withdrawal hit him with the impact of a fist. She had retreated into her shell again, battened down the hatches. She turned and went into the bathroom. He didn't try to stop her. In a moment he heard the shower. He picked up his swim trunks and shirt from the floor and went back to his own room to get ready for dinner. He wasn't going to let it go that easily. Whether she wanted to talk about it or not, they would talk at dinner.

He waited until they had finished eating and poured the last of the wine from the carafe into their glasses. Their table was on an outdoor terrace, overlooking the water. The light was soft and romantic; it highlighted the clinging pink material of April's dress, particularly over the thrust of her breasts, so that it appeared to have been dipped in silver.

"Now," Vic said, sitting back in his chair with the bowl of his glass cupped in one hand, "you can explain to me what you meant when you said you didn't want to talk about marriage."

There had been a small tremor in the pit of April's stomach since they had left the hotel because she had known that Vic wouldn't let the subject drop. He was only waiting for the right moment to bring it up again. With his words the tremor increased to a small quaking. She had to make him understand. "My marriage imprisoned me in an intolerable situation," she said quietly. "I've been totally disillusioned by the institution." She leaned toward him, adding earnestly, "Vic, I don't need a piece of paper."

He drained his glass and set it on the table. "Marriage is more than a piece of paper," he said, his voice sounding strained. "If two people are really in love, they want to make a commitment to each other."

Could he possibly doubt that she loved him? "Oh, darling, I do love you. I wouldn't be here with you if I didn't."

"Then marry me."

Nervously she clenched her hands together on the tabletop. Why must he persist in this? Only tonight had she found the golden depths of her womanhood, but he was going to spoil it. "I can't. If you want me to say that I won't see anyone else, I'll say it. We can be together whenever you want, for as long as you want."

"Won't see anyone else!" Vic grated incredulously. "Well, thanks a whole hell of a lot! I'm not interested in dating you, April. I want marriage and children."

"If—if you want children, you'll have to have them with someone else." The words nearly tore her throat as they passed, it was so difficult to say them. "When Paul died I swore I'd never get trapped like that, ever again."

"I'm not Paul Dubois."

The words were even, dropped into the tropic stillness with precision. They were the cornerstone of their relationship, and yet she could not chance building a marriage on them.

Slumping, she covered her face with her hands for a moment. When she slid them down she said, "I didn't mean that. Oh, I'm not saying this very well. Please try to understand how I feel, Vic."

"I understand perfectly. You don't trust me enough to

make a commitment. And if you don't trust me, April, you don't love me. Because without trust there's no kind of love worthy of the name."

"That isn't true! You're the only man I've ever really loved, the only one I ever will love," she said desperately. "Oh, please, darling, can't we just be together and love each other and . . . see what happens?" It was the classic cop-out for people who feared commitment; she hated herself for having to say it.

He stared at her huge eyes in her anguished face for a moment. And slowly his anger died. He shouldn't have mentioned marriage so soon. She needed time to get used to the idea. She'd come a long way in the past twenty-four hours, but she hadn't come that far. So he would give her more time. "Let's go back to the hotel," he said curtly.

They made love again later that night, but it wasn't the same as before. April wept silently when it was over and Vic held her, but neither of them talked about the invisible boundary lines that had been drawn about their relationship.

Vic dropped her off at her apartment at seven Sunday evening. She went in, eager to see Rusty. But the apartment was unusually silent as she entered. The only light was in the kitchen.

She set her suitcase in the entry, calling, "Hey, where is everybody?"

Nan came out of the kitchen with a spatula in one hand. "Oh, you're back sooner than I expected. I phoned the airline earlier, and they said your flight would arrive at eight."

"We took an earlier flight." That had been April's idea.

139

In spite of her promises to herself, she had started to feel guilty about leaving Rusty with Nan all weekend. Nan turned back into the kitchen and April followed her. "Is Rusty asleep already?"

Vigorously Nan beat the batter in a large bowl for a moment before she said, "He's with his grandparents." She released the spatula and turned to face April. "I told Mr. Dubois that you hadn't said anything about Rusty spending the weekend with him and Mrs. Dubois. But he insisted that you wouldn't mind. April, I thought about calling your hotel, but I didn't want to bother you. Mr. Dubois said he'd buy Rusty one of those monster games he's been wanting. Of course, Rusty begged to go when his grandfather said that."

April's shoulders slumped as she went to the cabinet and got the teakettle. She ran water into it and set it on the range. "The monster game, huh? Bribery, pure and simple."

Nan was scraping the batter from the bowl into a floured loaf pan. "Well . . . Rusty didn't act like he wanted to go with his grandfather until Mr. Dubois mentioned the game."

"When did Noble come here?"

"Early Saturday morning. He asked for you, and when I said you were out of town he wanted to take Rusty."

April reached into an overhead cabinet for a cup and tea bag. "Did he want to know where I was?"

"Yes, but I just said I wasn't free to give out that information." Nan set the loaf pan in the oven.

April laughed, but without much humor. "I'll bet he loved that. I suppose he got the information out of Rusty."

"You told Rusty that you would be with Mr. Leyland?"

"Yes. I've always been totally honest with him, except when I thought the truth would hurt him too much." April's and Nan's gazes met for a speaking instant; both of them knew she was referring to the truth about Paul that she would never tell Rusty. Taking a deep breath, April went on. "I told him that Vic and I were going to St. Thomas for a couple of days. I even showed him the Virgin Islands on the map. When is Noble supposed to bring Rusty back?"

"After dinner, he said."

The kettle whistled, and April made her tea. "When they come, Nan, I'd like you to leave Noble and me alone."

"Yes, ma'am," said Nan pertly, her eyes snapping. She clearly resented Noble's taking Rusty without permission as much as April did.

Noble brought Rusty home at nine thirty. Rusty burst into the apartment yelling, "Mom!"

She swooped him into her arms and hugged him tightly. "I missed you," she murmured into her son's tousled red hair. He smelled of the peppermint candy that Anna always kept in a dish in the living room. She held him away from her a little so that she could look into his freckled face.

"Grandpa bought me a monster game," Rusty said breathlessly. "Did you bring me back some seashells like you promised?"

"A whole sack full."

"You didn't buy them in a store, did you?"

April shook her head. "Nope. I picked them up at the beach."

Rusty grinned delightedly. "Good." For some unaccountable reason Rusty was convinced that shells from the beach were more authentic than shells from a store.

For the first time, April looked past Rusty at Noble. He'd dropped Rusty's overnight bag on a chair and was watching the scene with evident impatience. April straightened and said to Rusty, "I put the shells on your dresser. You go and look at them. I'll be there after I talk to Grandpa."

Rusty ran to give Noble a hug, then skipped from the room. "Sit down, Noble," April said. He hesitated momentarily, then strode to the sofa.

April perched on the arm of a chair. "I was surprised when I got home and learned that you'd taken Rusty for the weekend. You know I want you to clear his visits in advance with me."

Noble had that rigid set to his chin that meant he was furious. "You weren't here. I thought he'd be better off with his grandparents than with the housekeeper."

April felt herself getting angry. She made an effort to speak calmly. "Nan loves Rusty, and she takes excellent care of him. But that isn't the point. I made what I felt were the best arrangements for Rusty. You had no right to countermand my decision."

Two red spots had appeared high on Noble's cheeks. "You left Rusty alone to go off with a man! If I hadn't dropped by here unexpectedly—"

April's fingernails bit into the upholstered arm of the chair. She interrupted Noble. "Now, just a minute. Where I spent the weekend is none of your business."

"When it affects Rusty, it is," he stated flatly. "Did you really think I wouldn't find out?"

"You pumped Rusty for information! That's unforgivable, Noble!"

"Nobody had to pump Rusty." His mouth twisted as if he had tasted something rotten. How could she have forgotten how self-righteous Noble was? "The poor little boy was unhappy because his mother had left him to fly off on a clandestine weekend with Vic Leyland."

"Will you stop! There was nothing clandestine about it."

Noble went on as if she hadn't spoken. "When Anna asked him why he looked so sad, the whole story just poured out of him."

April knew that this was not what had happened. Anna had fawned and cried and asked Rusty questions about Vic until he had told her what she wanted to know to shut her up. She could hear Anna now. *Poor sweetheart, poor little fatherless boy . . .*

"Anna was so distressed that she begged me not to bring him back here. In the end, I had to tear him from her arms."

"Oh, God," April mumbled. In exasperation she jumped to her feet and faced Noble, her hands on her hips. "Let's get something understood right now. I told Rusty exactly where I was going and with whom. He wasn't upset about it when I left here. If he was later, you and Anna can take the credit for it."

His narrow-eyed scrutiny was frigid. "Apparently, April, I don't know you as well as I thought I did. I can't believe you can stand there boldly and admit that you're having a disreputable love affair right under the nose of your son!"

April clenched her teeth and her hands simultaneously. "I'm not having anything under Rusty's nose! And

143

whatever my relationship with Vic is, it's certainly not disreputable. How dare you preach to me, Noble Dubois! I'm a grown woman. I won't be dictated to!"

A flash of rage widened his eyes and flared his nostrils. He got to his feet and said with a deliberate intent to wound, "You were judged unfit to care for Rusty once, April. Evidently that situation hasn't improved as much as Anna and I had hoped." He walked past her toward the door.

She stared at his rigid back, stunned. "What do you mean by that?"

He turned at the door. "I mean I'll do whatever I have to to make sure that my grandson has the proper upbringing, and the way you are carrying on with Vic Leyland isn't proper, in my opinion."

"Your opinion! Your opinion is not the determining factor here. I make the decisions about Rusty's welfare."

"For now."

"Are you threatening to sue me for Rusty's custody?"

At the threshold he turned back to say, "It's an option that I'm keeping open." He let himself out as April watched, too angry and frustrated to respond.

After a few minutes she got herself in hand well enough to go in to Rusty. They looked through the bag of seashells together before he had his bath. She tucked him in, heard his prayer, and went back to the living room to sit in the dark and try to think where her conversation with Noble had gone wrong.

Nan found her there a while later. "Would you like something to eat before I go to bed?"

April peered up at Nan in the dimness. "He's going to try to take Rusty away from me," she said with such a frightened dullness in her tone that it twisted Nan's heart.

The housekeeper sat down beside April on the couch. She put a plump arm around her slumped shoulders. "He's just bluffing, honey. He can't take Rusty."

April shivered, although the room was warm. "He did it once."

"That was different," Nan soothed. "Rusty's father was alive then to assume custody. Why, I'll tell the judge what a fine mother you are. Miss Pritchett would vouch for you, too, and I know there are others. Don't make yourself sick over Mr. Dubois's threats. I don't know what's come over that man."

April hugged herself, running her hands over her arms as she stared straight ahead for a moment. Then she said, "Nan, Noble isn't to take Rusty anywhere without my permission. If he tries, call me at work or wherever I am."

"All right, April. Now that I see what's come of this weekend, I'm sorry I didn't call you in St. Thomas when he came here Saturday morning."

"It wasn't your fault, Nan. Just make sure it doesn't happen again."

It was much later when April finally was able to sleep. She wanted so much to phone Vic and seek his reassurance. But she couldn't, not after rejecting his marriage proposal. If she couldn't commit to marriage, then she had no right to lean on Vic when things got rough.

By the next evening she was feeling calmer. Nan was probably right. Noble was bluffing. But at dinner Rusty told her something that resurrected all her fears.

"Grandma came to school today," he said.

A thrill of trepidation oozed through April's veins. "Anna? What was she doing there?"

"She said she wanted to see me. It was at recess, and she made me stop playing soccer to sit in the car with her." Rusty's hazel eyes were troubled. "Mom, why does Grandma cry all the time?"

"I don't know, sweetheart," April said carefully. "Was she crying when you saw her today?"

"She wasn't at first. But when we got in the car she started. It was so loud, I thought the other kids would hear her. And she kept calling me her poor baby. I'm not a baby!"

"Of course you're not."

She watched Rusty take a bite of meatloaf, her insides quivering with alarm, wanting to ask him to tell her every word that Anna had uttered. But she mustn't frighten him. Oh, God, she needed Vic's strength at that moment.

Finally Rusty said, "She said I could come and live with her and Grandpa, but I told her I didn't want to. Then she said I didn't love her and started to cry again."

"What did you do then?"

"I said I loved her, but I loved you more and, besides, kids aren't supposed to live with their grandmas and grandpas." All at once his expression was sad. "Mom, Grandma acts so funny sometimes. It kinda scares me."

April kept her tone as matter-of-fact as she could. "You needn't be afraid of your grandmother, Rusty. And I don't think she'll come to your school again."

"I hope not," he confessed. "All the other kids made fun when I said I had to go with my grandma."

The next morning April paid a call on the principal of Rusty's school. When she left she had his promise that no one would be allowed to take Rusty off the school

146

grounds without her permission. He would inform Rusty's teachers, he promised. He seemed concerned that Rusty had left the yard the day before without being seen by the teacher who had playground duty. That teacher would get a lecture, April was sure.

She didn't hear from Vic for three days. Between worrying about what Noble and Anna would do next and wondering why Vic hadn't called, it was hard to keep her mind on the boutique. Fortunately they were in the midst of the winter slump and business was slow.

When Vic finally did call on Thursday morning she was so glad to hear his voice that, sitting at her desk in the office at the boutique, she grinned like a deprived child with a bright, new toy.

"Can you get away for dinner this evening?" he asked.

"Yes," she breathed. Then she decided to heck with pride and blurted out, "Oh, Vic, I'm so glad to hear your voice. When you didn't call, I thought that you might be angry with me."

"I'm not angry," he said quietly. "I've been snowed under at work the past few days. And I thought we both needed a little while to—er, come to grips with our situation. April, is something else bothering you?"

She should have known that she couldn't hide anything from Vic. All her staunch resolutions about handling her own problems crumpled as she heard the concern in his voice. "Yes. I—oh, Vic, I've cried on your shoulder enough."

"I don't think this can wait until tonight," he decided. "We'll go to lunch. I'll pick you up at the boutique at noon."

Since both of them needed to get back to work in an hour, they went to a restaurant in the Forum. As they ate club sandwiches April told him about her confrontation with Noble Sunday night. As she talked she fiddled nervously with every piece of cutlery in front of her. Finally both Vic's hands closed over one of her agitated hands, enclosing it in warmth and calmness.

"Don't let him do this to you, love."

She closed her eyes for a long moment while she tried to calm the furious beating of her heart. Telling Vic about it had brought back her fear of Sunday night with all its strength. "Vic . . ." She opened her eyes and looked at him with such despair. "What if I can't stop him?"

"I'm talking about the state you're in," he said quietly. "You won't be any help to yourself or Rusty if you don't get hold of yourself."

She knew that he was right. She had to be strong for Rusty. "As if Noble's insults weren't enough," she said, "Anna went to Rusty's school Monday, took him to her car, and carried on like a crazy woman. She's always been emotional, but she's acting like somebody on the verge of a nervous breakdown. It scares Rusty. I went to the school and told the principal that Rusty wasn't to leave the school ground again without my permission. He promised to keep a closer watch on him."

Vic looked disturbed. "The woman doesn't sound quite normal," he mused. "That's even more reason for you to keep her away from Rusty."

"Nan thinks Noble is bluffing about taking this to court, but I wish I could be sure. I've hardly slept for the past three nights."

Vic had finished his sandwich; April had eaten less than half of hers. "Aren't you going to eat that?"

She shook her head. "I'm not hungry."

"Come on then." He paid the check and walked with

148

her back to the boutique. At the door he took her in his arms and kissed her, disregarding the curious glances of the passersby. She was trembling, and when he lifted his head there were tears in her eyes. He took out his handkerchief and gently blotted the moisture from her eyes. "I'll find out if Noble's serious about going to court," he promised. "His attorney is a personal friend of mine, and he owes me a favor. I'll try to get in touch with him this afternoon."

"Thank you." She smiled at him mistily, her gratitude in her eyes. "Will you let me cook dinner for you tonight?"

She still stood in the circle of his arms. "Yes," he muttered as he took the opportunity to kiss her temple where wisps of hair escaped her chignon. He nuzzled her ear.

She laughed softly as a passing elderly woman frowned her disapproval. "We're creating a scandal."

He let her go reluctantly. "Is seven all right for dinner?"

"Perfect." She left him and entered the boutique, feeling somewhat better than when she had left for lunch. Vic would know what to do about Noble. It occurred to her that she was allowing herself to lean on Vic's strength, that she and Rusty were becoming much too entangled in his life, and that it wasn't exactly fair to him.

She heard Val in the storeroom. April went to her office and, standing at the window, looked down at the busy street below. The truth was she needed Vic right now. If she was going to take on Noble Dubois, she would need all the help she could get.

* * *

"Did you talk to Noble's lawyer?" The words April had been wanting to ask all evening burst from her as she and Vic settled into the living room couch. They'd had dinner with Rusty and, afterward, the three of them had played the monster game until Rusty's bedtime. Finally Nan had taken him off to bed, and April and Vic were alone.

Vic put out a hand, sliding his strong fingers around her neck and tugging gently. She resisted, intent upon having an answer to her question. His mouth turned down wryly. "I talked to him. I reminded him that he owed me a favor for a deal I sent him two years ago. Still, I had to use every persuasive argument I could think of to get anything out of him, but eventually he talked. I gave him my word that the source of my information would remain a secret. It mustn't go beyond the two of us, April."

"All right," she cried impatiently. "Just tell me what he said."

"Noble has talked to him about suing for Rusty's custody."

April's face paled. "Oh, God! I knew he would do it!"

His fingers on her nape moved in a slow motion while he eyed her thoughtfully. Finally he said, "He's using our relationship as an excuse to take you to court."

She eyed him warily. "Can he do that?"

Vic shrugged. "Anyone can sue anybody, I guess. But I don't think the judge will see you as an unfit mother on the basis of that alone, not in this day and age."

April stared up at him. "Well, I can't take any chances," she wailed softly. Her eyes filled with pain that told him how much it cost her to say the words. "We have to stop seeing each other, Vic."

150

"It wouldn't make any difference," he said, exerting enough pressure on her nape to draw her closer.

"It might. . . ." April broke off. She lowered her head to stare at Vic's sweatered chest.

"My friend got the idea that Anna is the real reason Noble is considering taking this to court. Apparently he's worried sick about her emotional state. Noble thinks that taking care of Rusty would pull her out of it."

"But that's incredible!" April exploded. "No judge would take a child away from his mother and give him to an unstable grandmother!"

He met her eyes as she raised her face to gaze up at him desperately. "Not if you could prove that Anna is unstable. It wouldn't be easy to get that kind of medical testimony."

"Oh, Vic, what am I going to do?"

"I think the first thing you have to do is get Rusty away from here. If Anna's as bad as Noble fears, she could do something drastic, like intercept Rusty at school and run away with him."

She gasped and Vic lowered his mouth to hers in a quick hot kiss to silence her. "I have it all figured out, love. You and Rusty can stay at my ranch until we can find out if Noble's going through with this and what's being done about Anna."

"Oh, Vic . . . Rusty's school . . . the business . . ." But her voice died as she realized that none of that mattered if Rusty was really in any danger. "I suppose I could leave Val in charge of the boutique for a few days. And I could get Rusty's school assignments from his teacher. . . ."

"Good. That's settled. I'll drive you down tomorrow morning."

"Thank you. I don't know how I'd handle this without you, Vic."

He bent his head to her anxious mouth and followed the outline of her lips with his tongue. A small sigh escaped April. "Forget Noble and Anna Dubois for tonight, love," he whispered as his thumb applied a gentle pressure at the corner of her mouth.

"Oh, Vic . . ."

"Shh . . . I'm going to make love to you," he whispered against her mouth. "Try to relax and enjoy it."

Her lips parted on a sigh of surrender as his tongue plunged hungrily between her lips. His hands came up to cradle her head and hold her immobile as he drank his fill of the warm honey he found in her mouth.

April felt the weakening heat of her response traveling along her veins. *Tomorrow,* she thought dazedly. *Tomorrow I'll worry about Rusty.* Vic let his hands glide down the length of her back in a slow, caressing touch that molded her breasts to his chest.

Under the spiraling rise of her own excitement and desire April freed her mouth to press it against his throat. She felt him tremble as she strung small kisses down to where the open collar of his shirt covered the ribbed edge of his sweater. When he groaned, his lips in her hair, April wound her arms around his neck. "Take me to bed, Vic."

He needed no further invitation. Standing, he scooped her from the couch and carried her to her bedroom, kicking the door shut behind them with his foot. "When I feel you come alive with passion in my arms, I can't tell you what it does to me, love," he muttered hoarsely as he set her on the bed and began undressing her. "To think that

I'm the one who set you free from the lies and self-doubt. It humbles me, my darling."

April lifted her heavy lashes at his words. She looked up at him with wonder in her dark eyes. "I need you so much, Vic . . . so much." Her voice broke. Her hands went to his belt and she released the buckle. She felt him shiver as her fingers slipped beneath the waistband of his trousers to tug the hook-fastening loose. "Love me, Vic. Oh, please . . ."

With frantic hands he succeeded finally in releasing them from the confinement of their clothing. With a groan he brought his body down on hers and she felt the surging strength of his manhood.

"Ah, April! I've been half out of my mind these past three days, remembering St. Thomas . . . wanting you again . . ."

"Vic, oh, Vic!"

Her body arched upward against his strength and he cupped her hips in his hands, and with a single, unleashed thrust, he entered her.

"I love you . . . I love you."

Their breathless voices mingled as they both said the words, and then Vic's mouth fastened on hers as they moved together in the age-old rhythm of love. Quickly the waves took them, rolling over them until there was nothing in the world for April but the man above her and the tender, thrilling, dizzying rapture they shared.

CHAPTER NINE

"Are we almost there, Vic?"

Rusty had been asking the same question every five minutes since they had left Tulsa at eight that morning. Now it was almost ten, and he was fidgeting all over the backseat of the car. To April's relief, Rusty had accepted without too many questions her explanation that the two of them were going on a short vacation and that Vic had invited them to stay at his ranch. She'd called Rusty's teacher before leaving and arranged to have Rusty's assignments mailed to the apartment. Nan was the only one who knew where April and Rusty would be staying, and she would forward the assignments to them. April had simply told Val that she had to leave town for a few days and would be in touch with her at the boutique by phone. Val had taken the news with equanimity, saying, "Don't worry about the boutique. I can handle it." Once again, April had thought, Thank heaven for Val Winston!

"We'll be there soon, Rusty," Vic said.

Rusty pressed his nose against the back window. "I gotta go to the bathroom."

"Not again," April murmured, giving Vic a wry look.

"You can go in a minute, old buddy," Vic said. "The ranch starts at that corner post we just passed. The house is about a quarter mile up this road."

It was a big, white, two-story with Victorian gingerbread trim outlining the eaves and open front porch. "It was built at the turn of the century," Vic said as he pulled into a curving gravel drive. "It's inconveniently arranged and drafty, typical of ranch houses built then in this part of the country. I've added storm windows and insulation. But if it weren't for the wood we cut off the ranch and burn in the two fireplaces, the heating bill would be astronomical."

"Oh, Vic," April breathed, "I love it."

He caressed her cheek with the back of his hand, his eyes approving. He stopped the car next to the house in front of a detached white triple-car garage, clearly of more recent origin than the house. There were rooms above the garage with an outside stairway leading up to them.

Rusty scrambled out of the backseat as soon as the car came to a stop. "Where're the horses?"

"Probably out to pasture," Vic said. "We'll go hunt them up after lunch."

A large collie bounded around the corner of a red barn about a hundred yards from the house, halted as he saw them, then tore toward Vic, yelping happily. Vic stooped and caught the squirming dog in his arms, rubbing his neck and behind his ears. "This is Lieutenant, better known as Looey," he said. "Come and say hello."

After April and Rusty were properly introduced to Lieutenant, Vic put one arm around April and the other hand on Rusty's shoulder and they walked toward the house, with Looey barking excitedly at their heels. The front door flew open just as they reached it. A short, fat, red-haired woman wearing a checked bib apron over overalls and a man's flannel shirt, cried, "Come in, come in! Mr. Vic, you're a sight for sore eyes, you are!" She hugged Vic's neck, then turned to Rusty. "This has to be

156

Rusty. I've got a big glass of milk and warm brownies waitin' for you, lad."

They followed the robust Rosie inside, and Vic said, "Rosie, this is April Dubois. April, meet my housekeeper, Rosie Plimpton." Rosie put her hands on her ample hips and surveyed April with a broad smile. "Howdy do, Miz Dubois. Sam and me have been expectin' you all morning."

"We couldn't get away until eight, Rosie," Vic said with a dry chuckle. To April, he added, "Rosie thinks the day's half gone by then. Sam, by the way, is Rosie's husband. He's the ranch foreman. This place would fall to rack and ruin in about a week without Rosie and Sam."

Rosie grinned at him. "It's sure nice to be appreciated. Well, come on back to the kitchen. I've got a fresh pot of coffee on. Sam's out to the barn, doctoring that young roan gelding. He tried to walk through a barbed wire fence and tore a gash in his leg. The gelding, not Sam." The last was added with a quick grin over her shoulder.

She was talking as they walked through a large, square living room with a floor-level brick fireplace on one wall. Logs were burning behind a brass fire screen. The pine floor gleamed with wax. A red and blue braided rag rug covered about half the room on the fireplace side. A huge navy leather couch faced two red corduroy armchairs in front of the fireplace.

They had reached the kitchen. It was almost as large as the living room, high-ceilinged, with gleaming white cabinets and appliances along two walls and a round oak table surrounded by six ladder-back chairs arranged in the center of the red-brick linoleum. A second brick fireplace, smaller than the one in the living room, occupied one corner. A cast iron kettle hung on a hook over burning logs. Rosie got a potholder and stirred the pinto beans and ham hocks in the kettle. "In wintertime, I always fix beans and cornbread on Friday nights," she said.

"That, Rosie, is why we picked today to arrive," Vic teased as he pulled out a chair for April.

Rosie chuckled. "None too soon either. Can you believe it's March already? We won't be needin' the fires more'n another week or two."

"Is the gelding healing all right?" Vic asked.

Rosie put the lid back on the kettle and reached for the coffeepot. "He is now. Had a little infection the first few days. Sam had Doc Varner take a look at him. Doc gave him a shot, and Sam's been putting on salve twice a day. It looks a whole lot better than it did a week ago."

Rusty stood in front of the fireplace, his hands in his jeans pockets. He had been following this exchange with interest. "What's a gelding, Vic?"

Rosie laughed, her eyes crinkling shut and her double chin bouncing. "Law, you can sure tell he's a city child, can't you?"

"A gelding's a boy horse, Rusty," Vic said, taking the chair next to April's and catching her eye with a grin.

"Like a stallion, you mean?" Rusty asked, clearly proud that he knew the proper name for a male horse.

Vic coughed as Rosie set a big mug of steaming coffee in front of him and winked wickedly. "Not exactly. A gelding can't breed the mares because he's been cut—er, operated on." April grabbed her coffee mug and lifted it to her face to hide her smile. Vic didn't miss it, though, and he tossed her a silent, narrow-eyed warning.

Thankfully Rosie put a glass of milk and a plate of brownies on the table at that moment, diverting Rusty's attention. Unbuttoning his down-filled jacket, he climbed into a chair and reached for a brownie. "Can I go down to the barn after I drink my milk?"

"Sure," Vic said. "We'll all go."

Rusty proceeded to stuff a brownie into his mouth and gulp down his milk. Before April and Vic had finished their coffee, he announced, "I'm ready. Let's go."

Seeing Rusty wasn't going to give them any peace until he'd seen the barn and the injured gelding, April and Vic finished their coffee quickly, put their jackets back on, and headed for the barn with Rusty running ahead of them. Lieutenant ran by Rusty's side, wagging his tail and barking.

Looking up at the garage apartment, April asked, "Do Sam and Rosie live over the garage?"

"Yep." Vic reached for her hand, placing it with his into the deep pocket of his jacket. "I wish I could stay longer, but at least we'll have the house all to ourselves tonight." Vic had to return to Tulsa Saturday evening to make connections with a flight to California early Sunday morning. He was to speak at an energy seminar the following week.

"You're forgetting about Rusty," April reminded him.

"No, I'm not. I've been dreaming of getting you and Rusty down here for a long time."

Despite her underlying anxiety over what Noble was up to back in Tulsa, April felt a bright sting of pleasure. "Rusty loves it already."

"What about you?"

She gazed out over the flat brown grassland surrounding the ranch buildings. A line of willows marked the horizon; the creek Vic had mentioned must lie in that direction. No other house was in sight. Soon the grass

159

would be greening, the trees budding. It must be beautiful here in the spring. "It's so peaceful," she said. "How could I help but like it?"

Vic was elated. He suddenly realized that he'd been worried over her reaction to his beloved ranch. Deep in his pocket, his hand squeezed hers. "This is my real home. The town house is just a place where I eat and sleep when I'm in the city. After lunch I want to show every corner of it to you. It will probably take all afternoon. Do you ride?"

"No," she said apologetically, feeling that she was disappointing him.

"That's okay. We'll take the jeep."

In the barn, a tall, skinny man in faded jeans, a denim jacket, and scuffed cowboy boots was closing the gate on a stall at the far end. He tipped his western hat back on his head, exposing curly brown hair, and grinned as they approached.

The collie ran off to sniff out the corners of the barn, and Vic introduced April and Rusty to his foreman. Then he asked, "How's the gelding, Sam?"

"He's gonna be okay."

Rusty looked up Sam's long length, his eyes wide. "Are you a real cowboy, Mr. Plimpton?"

Sam grinned and laid his rough, callused hand on Rusty's red hair. "I reckon I am, Rusty."

"Where's your lasso?"

Sam threw back his head and cackled. "I got one back in the tack room. I hear you're gonna be here a few days. Would you like me to teach you to rope?"

"Golly, would you?" Rusty's eyes were as big as silver dollars. "Vic said maybe you'd teach me to ride a horse too."

160

"I 'spect we can do a little of both."

"Can I see the gelding now?"

"Why, you sure can." Sam picked up Rusty and held him so that he could see over the top of the stall. "We better not go in right now. I just doctored 'im and he's kinda nervous."

Behind them, Vic put his arm around April and, pulling her close to his side, whispered in her ear, "Have I told you today that I love you?"

Leaning against him, April looked up at him, flushing, her bottom lip caught between her teeth in what Vic thought was charming embarrassment. "No," she murmured.

His look lingered dreamily on her mouth for an instant before he bent to kiss her earlobe and whisper throatily, "I love you, April Dubois."

When it dawned upon April that Sam and Rusty had turned and were watching them, she asked quickly, "What's Looey barking at?"

The dog was at the back of the barn, looking up at a crude shelf that ran along the wall. Sam tugged his hat back down on his forehead. "He's discovered that old Pirate's home."

Rusty laughed and ran toward the collie. "Look, Mom, it's a squirrel!"

As April and Vic followed Rusty she saw a big wire cage on the shelf. Inside the cage a squirrel sat eating something that he held in his paws. The squirrel studied them, bright-eyed, and made its skittering, barking sound. Then, in a flash, he darted through the open cage door and leaped onto Vic's shoulder.

Rusty squealed with delight as Vic stroked the squirrel's coat. "You always come back when you get hungry,

161

don't you, Pirate?" The squirrel darted behind Vic's head and sat on his other shoulder, cocking his head at April and Rusty.

April put out a tentative hand, but Pirate darted out of reach, back to Vic's other shoulder. "He'll let you touch him when he gets to know you," Vic said.

"How did you tame him?" April asked.

"I found him, half-starved, when he was a baby. His mother had disappeared, probably killed by a coyote or a hawk. I brought him back to the house and Rosie hand-fed him until he got so impudent he was pilfering every small, bright object in sight. He's a real thief. That's how he got his name. Anyway, when Rosie lost her thimble—and her temper—Sam built this cage and Pirate was banished to the barn."

"But the cage door is open," Rusty said.

"It's always been open," Vic told him. "This was never intended to be anything but a place where Pirate could be warm and dry and get away from Looey. Rosie keeps a mixture of nuts, dried fruit, and seeds in his dish there, and he comes and goes as he pleases."

Pirate crawled down to Vic's chest, flipping his tail, and Rusty eyed him longingly, clearly eager to touch him. "Aren't you afraid he'll run away and never come back?"

"No," Vic said. "This is his home for as long as he wants. I'd feel sad if Pirate decided not to come back, but that's his choice and I'd respect it." As he spoke, Vic's gaze had locked with April's. She realized suddenly that his words were meant to apply to more than to Pirate. "Not even an animal should be forced to stay where he doesn't want to be. If he couldn't leave when he wanted to, it wouldn't be a home. It would be a prison."

April flushed as she understood Vic's deeper meaning. *Don't let him make you forget what it was like with Paul,* she warned herself. Things can happen that circumvent the best of intentions. She quickly averted her eyes. "I think I'll go back to the house and see if I can help Rosie with lunch."

She left Rusty with the two men in the barn and hurried back to the house.

As April came in, Rosie was turning pieces of fried chicken in a skillet on the range. April hung her jacket on a rack on the enclosed back porch and entered the kitchen. "I came back to see if I could help you," April said.

"Why, that's mighty nice of you, Miz Dubois, but—"

"Call me April. Please."

Rosie set a lid over the chicken and turned to run curious green eyes over April's slender, blue-jeaned figure. "All right, April. And if you're bound and determined to help, you can set the table and make the salad."

Within moments the two women were working comfortably together. "I gotta tell you," Rosie said, "after meeting you, I'm real relieved."

"Relieved?"

"Well, I had this mental picture of the women Mr. Vic associates with in the city. Fancy dressers, you know. Snooty. But you're not like that at all."

"Thank you, Rosie."

Standing at the stove, Rosie looked over her shoulder at April. Her green eyes were warm and appraising. "Maybe that's why he thinks so much of you. You're not like the others."

"Oh? How do you know how Vic feels about me?"

"Why, he never brought a woman out here before.

163

Since I know how much he loves this place, I know he wouldn't have brought you here if you weren't important to him."

"Did Vic tell you why Rusty and I are staying for a few days?"

"No, ma'am. It's none of my business. I'm just glad to have the two of you, and I'll do my best to make you feel at home."

April returned the woman's smile. "Rosie, Vic once told me you were a big-hearted woman. Now I understand what he meant."

After lunch Sam took Rusty with him to feed the horses and April and Vic set out in the jeep. The day was still cold, with the ever-present wind blowing from the northeast. The Oklahoma sky was a cloudless, pale blue. April looked out over the seemingly endless, rolling pastureland and thought that the man at her side fit remarkably well with the country. In faded jeans, a flannel shirt, a deerskin jacket, and western boots, Vic looked completely the rancher. She looked at his strong hands gripping the steering wheel; at the moment it was difficult to imagine him behind a desk in a corporate office or speaking to four hundred participants in a seminar. She was beginning to perceive how varied were the aspects of Vic's personality.

"Have you ever considered drilling for oil on the ranch?" she asked.

"I've had my geologists do a survey. If there's anything here, it's so deep that it wouldn't be feasible to drill for it at today's prices." He brought the jeep to a halt at a wide, metal gate and leaped out. "Drive through for me."

The wind whipped into the jeep with Vic when he returned, and April hunched her shoulders so that the turned-up collar of her jacket partly covered her ears. Vic slammed the door. "I should have found a cap for you. We may have to walk a ways to find the horses."

April dug her gloves out of her pockets and put them on. "I'll be fine. I'm tougher than you seem to think, Vic Leyland."

Vic's heart missed a beat. She might have to be tough these next few weeks. Opening his jacket, he pulled her against him, wrapping the jacket around her. Her arms slipped around his waist, resting against the warmth of his body. Vic's mouth was in her hair. "Tough, huh?" he muttered. "You feel pretty soft to me."

April remained quietly in his arms, turning her cheek against his chest. "You make me feel so safe," she whispered. "Rosie and Sam and this place—and, most of all, you—it makes me feel as though nothing bad could possibly happen to me."

His arms tightened around her. "Nothing bad will happen if I have anything to say about it." He bent to brush his lips across her forehead; she lifted her face and he placed a hard, cold kiss upon her upturned mouth.

"What are we going to do?" she said thickly when the kiss ended. He knew that she was referring to Rusty; though she had been trying valiantly all day to push the worries out of her mind, she had never fully succeeded. He had also noticed that she'd said "we" and not "I." Whether she realized it or not, she was starting to think of the two of them as a team. At least this is what Vic told himself.

April breathed a little sigh and bowed her head so that her forehead almost touched his chin.

"I've been thinking about that."

"Have you come up with any answers?" she said from beneath her hair.

"One. A private investigator."

She lifted her head. He raised his hands and pushed back the disheveled locks from her face.

She looked deep into his eyes. "To try to get something on Noble, you mean?"

"No, to follow Anna. She's the weak link. We know that she's seeing a psychiatrist, but for court we need dates, times, and anything else we can get to prove that she's unstable."

Her eyes suddenly filled with tears. "Oh, Vic, that seems so—so ungrateful. Anna was always good to me."

"Honey, if you want to protect Rusty, you're going to have to fight fire with fire. If we can get proof of Anna's instability, the mere threat of using it in court might be enough to make Noble back off. I know a good investigator. He can go to work on it Monday."

A sudden lash of wind shrieked by them, rocking the jeep. She shivered against him, laying her head on his shoulder, hugging his waist. "We have to do it, don't we?"

"Yes."

She was silent for a moment. Finally she said, "All right. Tell me how to get in touch with him."

"I'll call him at home Sunday when I'm in town."

"Thank you."

"April?"

She lifted her head to look into his eyes. "What, Vic?"

"If we were married, Rusty would have a home with both a mother and a father. Noble wouldn't have a leg to stand on in court."

"That isn't any reason to get married," she whispered.

166

"No," he said so quietly that she could barely hear him. He cupped her face in his large hands and gazed into her eyes for a long time. "The only reason for any two people to get married is because they love each other and want to spend the rest of their lives together."

He made it sound so simple, April thought, as they trudged across the pasture in search of the horses. And there at the ranch with Vic, it seemed almost simple. She was cold and tired from their long walk into the wind, but at the same time contented. Vic wanted to marry her. It wasn't so much that she had changed her mind about marriage—she hadn't really—it was just that it made her happy to know that Vic wanted to make the commitment.

He enjoyed having her with him, showing her the ranch, talking to her about the horses. It was obvious in the way he slowed his long-legged stride so that she wouldn't have to run to keep up with him, and in the way he put his arm around her occasionally and smiled down at her when neither of them had said anything funny.

But she was glad that he didn't mention marriage again, even when they made love that night in the large oak bed in Vic's room, after Rusty, keyed up from his afternoon with Sam, had finally fallen asleep.

The big bedroom was cold, and Vic undressed her beneath layers of warm blankets. And then they were both naked in the dark, cozy cave of Vic's bed. Vic's hand sought her waist, and his fingers spread wide on her ribs, pulling her against him as he pressed his mouth into the curve of her neck, nuzzling her hair aside to kiss her nape.

"April," he whispered, "you're so soft and beautiful."

Her captive breath escaped her lungs with a fragile

moan. His tongue wet the warm hollow behind her ear until a tingle of excitement ran through her and her head fell forward. He kissed the soft skin of her neck and his hands slipped over the firm roundness of her breasts. He felt her shudder of pleasure and groaned with his own arousal.

She wound her arms around his neck. "Oh, Vic, you feel so good," she murmured against his naked shoulder.

"Not as good as you."

She entangled her legs with his, pressing against him, and felt the thrusting strength of his arousal against her stomach. His palms moved down her back, exploring quietly, arousing her with tenderness and care, appeasing her need to be touched and held. "My darling," she breathed, "I need this so much."

His husky voice beside her ear said, "I know. We both do." His hands played over her, fingering the narrow line of her backbone down to splay against her hips as they strained to be ever nearer.

Floating in a warm, deep enchantment, April's hands made their own exploration over his broad back, his rib cage, his taut, lean hips.

When their blanketed cave had grown hot with their excitement and their breathing was quick and labored and the sounds they murmured against smooth skin and moist mouths had become incoherent with passion, Vic shifted, fitting his hard strength into the welcoming softness of her body. Vic's groan was muffled in her hair as April gasped against his shoulder. As their bodies moved together in the harmony of desire, she reached for him with arms and legs, wrapping her love around him. To-

168

gether they glided down that golden path known only to true lovers toward the upward spiral of total abandon that plunged them, at last, into the pure, mindless rapture that comes with the perfect joining of body and soul.

CHAPTER TEN

During the next week the early spring days ran together for April. It was the timeless sort of idyll in which there were no appointments to keep and nothing was so urgent that it couldn't be put off until tomorrow. She reveled in the quiet, languid days, knowing that they wouldn't last.

Mornings, she helped Rosie in the kitchen or read a novel she had found in Vic's bedroom, where she slept alone in the oak bed. Each day at ten she phoned Val and conferred with her about the boutique. On Wednesday Val told her that warmer temperatures had brought more customers into the shop, and for the first time April felt guilty about leaving everything on Val's shoulders. But when she voiced her feelings, Val insisted, "You needed to get away. I didn't want to say anything before, but you've been jumpy lately. I don't know what's troubling you, April, but stay and get it worked out. We're managing fine here."

Every morning Sam took Rusty out for "bronco bustin' and ropin' lessons," as Sam called it. He'd brought a gentle old mare in from the pasture for Rusty to ride, and Rusty was in "hog heaven," another of Sam's expressions. Rusty adored Sam and followed him around the same way that Looey scampered at Rusty's heels.

Midweek, an envelope from Nan containing Rusty's assignments arrived. April and Rusty spent the early part of the afternoons, after that, on his schoolwork, over

Rusty's protests that he was going to be a cowboy, like Sam, and he didn't see why cowboys had to go to school. When Sam heard him, he spoke sternly, the only time April heard him do so all week: "Listen, little sidekick, I finished high school and I wanted to go on to college. But my dad thought an education was foolishness. He couldn't even read, and he was so poor when he died the county had to bury him. You oughta be glad your momma puts a high value on learnin' and encourages you like she does. You can be a cowboy, if you want to, but it's a far sight better to be a smart cowboy than a dumb one. Take my word for it."

April had no more trouble getting Rusty to do his assignments after that. And, each afternoon, after the schoolwork was finished, they walked along the bank of the meandering brown creek, with Looey at their heels. Rusty peered up into every tree they passed, looking for Pirate, whom they hadn't seen since the weekend.

One day Rusty said, "I hope he hasn't run away."

"He comes home at night," April said. "Sam says his food is gone each morning. He may be shy about coming around during the day because there are strangers about."

"You and me?" Rusty sounded indignant. "We wouldn't hurt him. Do you think he's found another home, someplace he likes better than here?"

"I doubt it."

"I wish Sam would lock him in his cage so I could make friends with him."

If he couldn't leave when he wanted to, it wouldn't be a home. It would be a prison. "He'll come back when he's ready. Animals want to be free, honey, just like people."

That night Vic called from San Francisco. The private

172

investigator was on the job, he told her, and maybe he'd have something for them by next weekend.

"Rusty and I can't stay here indefinitely," she said.

"I thought you liked the ranch."

"I love it, but this isn't our home."

"It could be."

She couldn't tell him that the same thought had occurred to her, that she'd even spent a few minutes earlier that day imagining how she'd remodel the kitchen if it were hers. Of course, as soon as she'd realized what she was thinking, she'd stopped herself. "I—I miss you."

"Me too. I know you're worried about the situation with Rusty, but I hope you're using some of your time at the ranch to think about us. You never had a real marriage with Paul, April. Real love doesn't cage people, it sets them free to be themselves." She thought about Pirate, who came home for sustenance and warmth and stroking and then left again to do whatever squirrels do in their wanderings.

"I don't know," she murmured unhappily. "I wish you were here."

"I'll be home Friday. I'm meeting with the investigator that morning in my office. I'll get away as early as I can."

"I'll be waiting."

A long silence hummed between them. She thought about going to bed alone and wished that Vic were there to hold her. The memory of their lovemaking Friday night evoked a rippling wave of desire.

"April?"

"Yes—I'm here."

"I want you. This very minute I want you so much I'm aching with it."

A flush of pleasure suffused her body. "Oh, Vic . . ."

173

She heard him draw in a huge breath before he said, "It's going to be a long night, sweetheart."

"For me too."

"Good night, love."

"Good night, Vic."

Later she lay awake in the darkness and reflected upon freedom and what it meant. Funny, but she hadn't really thought about it before she married Paul. She had loved her husband in the beginning; it was a naive, girlish love, but it was as much as she was capable of at the time. What she hadn't known then was how very fragile that kind of love could be. Long before her first wedding anniversary, she had stopped loving Paul. To survive, she had been forced to block off her feelings after they had been repeatedly battered by his insensitivity and cruelty. All of the tender emotions she allowed herself were channeled toward Rusty. He became her reason for living. No sacrifice had been too great for her son, even returning to her role as victim in a farce of a marriage.

Maybe what Vic said was true, that love freed people, but it could bind, too, as her love for Rusty had bound her to Paul.

Yet her love for Vic was real and deep, as her love for Paul had never been. Vic was compassionate and giving and he wanted her as his wife. But Vic was strong, too, and strong men had limits beyond which they would not go. Where were Vic's limits? How long would he be willing to continue in their present relationship? Did she even have a right to ask him to? But how could she possibly let him go?

Freedom. If she let Vic walk out of her life, things would be as they had been before, when she had thought she was free. Yes, things would be the same, but she would be different. Love bound in ways that had nothing to do with where a person happened to be, whether he was alone or with people. It bound the heart; it bound the soul. And she was just beginning to see the paradox in that. While it bound with tender ties, love liberated whatever was good and true in the lover. Love bound and freed at the same time.

Sighing, April turned over in the bed, hugging a pillow against her chest. To spend every weekend and holiday with Vic at the ranch . . . to live with him in the town house . . . to grow old together. The thought both thrilled and frightened her. She could have it all, if she were willing to trust again, to risk.

She was no closer to making a decision when Vic returned Friday at one. Sam had taken Rusty into town with him in his pick-up to buy feed for the horses. April was in the kitchen with Rosie when she heard the car turn into the gravel drive.

"It's Vic!" she cried over her shoulder as she dashed outside. She didn't see Rosie's knowing smile.

The Cadillac was disappearing into the garage as she came out. She ran into Vic's arms just as he stepped out of the car.

He caught her against him, lifting her off the ground and swinging her around. "April—" he breathed. He let her body slide slowly down the length of his so that he could look into her eyes. "Oh, God, April, I thought I'd never get back here to you. I worked straight through last night just so I could get away early today. Has it really been only a week?"

She took his face in her hands—his wonderful, tired face with its strength and vulnerability. "No, it's been forever—at least." Standing on her toes, she kissed the tired lines beside his mouth.

And he caught her to him and placed his mouth over hers and kissed her with an almost desperate passion until she was dizzy and breathless and glowing.

She felt his heart pounding against her breast and his arms tighten around her with painful need, and when he released her mouth, she murmured against his neck, "I thought it was only a dream that you loved me."

He bent his head and muttered against her cheek, "If we had time, I'd show you right here and now how much I love you."

She smiled dreamily. "I've never made love in a Cadillac before."

He laughed deep in his throat. "By God, I'd do it if I weren't afraid Rosie would come out to see what's taking us so long." He lifted his head and looked down at her. "Anyway, we have to go back to Tulsa right away. I told Noble we'd be at his office at five."

"You *what?*"

"The investigator I hired tailed Anna all week. She went to see her psychiatrist every day at eleven. Noble drove her. We've got pictures of her entering and leaving. She looks terrible."

April shook her head sadly and bent her forehead to Vic's shoulder, thinking about Anna, who had lost the son she idolized and now wanted to replace him with April's son. Poor, desperate woman.

"The investigator questioned Anna's next door neighbor. The woman is apparently the neighborhood gossip. She knew all about Anna's emotional problems. She even gave the investigator some pretty weird examples of Anna's behavior lately. Once, it seems, Noble found her standing out in the street in the middle of the night in her nightgown. But not before several of the neighbors had seen her and come out to see what was happening. She was screaming that Noble had turned Paul against her and now Paul wouldn't come to see her anymore."

"Oh, Vic . . . how awful." She looked up at him, her dark eyes filled with pity. "Does Noble know that you've been investigating Anna?"

"No, that's what we're going to tell him at five."

Troubled lines furrowed her brow. "I don't think I could agree to this coming out in court, for everyone to know. No matter what Noble does. I still care deeply for Anna. It would be too cruel to do that to her."

"Then we have to stop it before it gets to court. We'll lay it all out for Noble and we have to make him believe we'll tell everything in open court if we have to."

Although Vic's strong arms and body surrounded April in warmth, she shivered suddenly. "I guess we don't have any other choice. While I change my clothes you can give Rosie some reason for our trip. Do you think she and Sam will mind keeping Rusty while we're gone?"

"I'm sure they won't."

"Oh, Vic, thank you for being here. I don't know if I could get through this alone."

"You don't have to get through it alone, love. You don't have to go through anything alone ever again."

He kissed her with infinite tenderness before they turned and, arm in arm, walked back to the house.

The Dubois Corporation's headquarters occupied three floors of a circular office tower in downtown Tulsa. April had been there only a few times when she was married to

Paul. As she and Vic entered the marble-floored reception area, it looked larger and colder than she remembered. And she had the same reaction to Noble as he stood up behind his huge walnut desk when she and Vic walked in.

"Where have you hidden Rusty?" Noble demanded.

April felt the familiar apprehension that Noble's righteous indignation always elicited in her. "Rusty and I have been away on vacation," she said, thankful for the pressure of Vic's hand at her waist.

"It's obvious you're trying to keep him away from Anna and me. You took him out of school without a word to anybody! This is just another example of your negligence, April. Rusty should be in school."

"Negligence! I—"

Vic interrupted, his voice low, determined. "Now, look here, Noble. I won't stand here and let you insult April. If you're willing to discuss this calmly, we'll stay. Otherwise, we'll leave right now."

The skin around Noble's mouth went white. It was the only indication of his anger as he said stiffly, "Sit down then, and say what you have to say."

Vic and April sat in two leather chairs facing Noble's desk. Noble looked at them calculatingly for a moment, then lowered himself into his chair. He sat forward and placed his forearms on the desk, as if bracing himself for a fight.

Vic sat straight in his chair, his hands resting on his spread knees. They look like two street fighters, April thought, tense and ready, each one waiting for the other to make the first move.

"It's about your threat to sue April for custody of Rusty," Vic said.

178

"I hope," April intervened, "that you've had second thoughts about that, Noble."

"I've had second thoughts, all right! Since you've taken Rusty out of school, I'm more convinced than ever that you aren't providing the proper environment for him."

"I've helped Rusty keep up with his schoolwork," April said. "He isn't falling behind his classmates."

"That isn't the point—"

"No, it isn't!" snapped Vic. "Is turning Rusty over to the care of an unstable woman your idea of the proper environment, Noble?"

Noble stiffened, and half-stood behind his desk. "How dare you, Leyland! If you're insinuating that my wife—"

Vic cut him off. "I'm not insinuating anything." He reached inside his jacket and pulled out the manila envelope containing the private investigator's report and the photographs of Anna entering and leaving her psychiatrist's office. "An investigator has been following your wife all week. Take a look."

Noble's face paled and his hands shook as he opened the envelope. For the first time since entering the office, April felt a twinge of pity for him. He drew out the papers and photographs and looked through them silently. Finally he crammed the envelope's contents back inside and tossed it to one side. "What is this supposed to prove?"

April touched Vic's arm to silence the blunt answer that she knew was coming. "Noble, I'm sorry that Anna is ill. I really am. But don't you see that even if you should win Rusty's custody it would be harmful for him to be with Anna now."

"This," said Noble sullenly, indicating the manila envelope, "isn't admissible evidence in court. A psychiatrist's case files are confidential."

"The fact that she is under the daily care of a psychiatrist is admissible," Vic said. "The neighbors can be called to testify to your wife's irrational behavior. And we'll ask to have an independent psychiatrist examine her and testify to his findings."

"I don't want to hurt Anna, Noble," April said quietly, "but I'll do what I have to if you take this to court." Nervously she stood and faced Noble. "I'll tell everything this time. We'll call Paul's mistresses to the stand. I'll tell about the times he beat me and left me so battered I was ashamed to leave the house for weeks. Nan and Elana will back me up on that. And Anna will hear every word."

Noble had clenched his hands into fists on the desk. He stared at her as if she had been transformed into somebody else before his eyes. "He didn't! Paul wouldn't . . ."

"He did, Noble! How long will you keep lying to yourself about Paul? He was a cruel, selfish man!"

"I have influence in this town," Noble sputtered.

Vic was watching April uneasily, knowing how much raw courage it took for her to stand up to Noble like this. He stood and put his arm around April. "I'm not without influence myself." They faced Noble, April's eyes pained, her chin thrust stubbornly forward, Vic's look boring into Noble, level and determined. "And I'm in this with April, all the way."

For the first time in April's experience Noble Dubois was faced with someone he considered an equal. She knew from Noble's fierce expression that he would have liked to destroy Vic on the spot. "You and April are

180

having an affair openly and seemingly without embarrassment," Noble clipped out, "and Rusty is the one who will be hurt by it."

"Nobody's going to be hurt," April said calmly. She looked at Vic and his arm tightened around her. And in that moment, all of her doubts were erased. Marriage to Vic would not be a trap. Like Pirate's cage in the barn, it would be the warm, loving, strong center of her life that would set her free to be the woman she wanted to be. "I'm going to marry Vic, if he'll have me. Then Rusty will have a home anybody would call proper."

She hadn't known she was going to say the words until the moment they were uttered, and she felt warmth suffusing her cheeks. Would Vic think she'd taken too much for granted? She looked into Vic's eyes. *I've been so wrong. Please say you still want me.*

Surprise flashed in Vic's eyes and was replaced by a warm glow of gratitude. For a moment they were lost in each other's gaze. Then Vic recovered himself and said, "That's right, Noble. We're getting married right away. So you won't have even the flimsiest grounds for taking April to court."

Slowly Noble stood up behind his desk. His face was deathly white, and April suspected that he was still thinking about what she'd said about Paul. Deep lines grooved his forehead and slashed from his nose to the corners of his mouth. She had never thought of Noble as old, but he looked old in that moment—like a battered, ancient warrior taking his first defeat at the hands of younger and stronger opponents. Suddenly he leaned over and braced himself against the desk, his head bowed.

"I thought if Anna could have Rusty, she might get

181

well." His voice was muffled. "Sometimes—lately—she doesn't even seem to know me. She thinks Paul's alive, that I'm keeping him from her somehow." He paused and released a trembly breath. "The doctor says she must be hospitalized. I have to accept it."

"Oh, Noble." Touched by his thick words, she went around the desk and put her hand on his shoulder. Tears wet her cheeks. "I'm sorry about Anna. You know I've always loved her. But with the proper care she'll get well. And when she's better I'll take Rusty to see her. You and Anna will always be Rusty's grandparents, and I want you to have a relationship with him."

Noble lifted his head. His eyes were red-rimmed. "You've won, April, but don't expect me to be gracious about it. Just go. Leave me alone."

She glanced at Vic, her eyes asking if they dared leave Noble alone like this. He nodded. "Come on," he said, taking her arm as they left the suite.

In the hall she said, "Oh, Vic, he looked so old and broken. I feel so sorry for him."

He put his arms around her, and she tipped her head back to look up at him. "Don't waste your pity. Noble will be on his feet and fighting tomorrow. He's not a man who dwells on his own past mistakes."

She sighed. "He's really hurting, Vic. He adores Anna, and it's killing him to see what's happening to her."

"From what you've told me, he probably contributed to it," Vic said. "He kept her sheltered and protected from life until Paul died. But he couldn't protect her from the pain of losing her only son, and she hadn't had any practice in coping with tragic reality."

"I know."

Vic's eyes held hers. "Did you mean what you said in there, about marrying me?"

Her eyes were shining with the glow of love. "I meant it. If you still want me."

"If! Haven't I been telling you how much I want you for weeks?"

She smiled up at him, her dark eyes overflowing with love. "Oh, Vic, take me somewhere and love me."

He kissed her then, a long, yearning kiss that sealed their commitment. He lifted his head and growled deep in his throat, "The town house. We'll call Rosie and tell her we won't be back until tomorrow. I'm not sharing you with anyone tonight, love."

The evening's gray shadows softened by moonlight fell upon the bed and wrapped itself around the lovers. Moments ago they had tumbled across the bed, fully clothed, so eager to be in each other's arms that all else was forgotten.

Lying on top of Vic, April lifted her head from his kiss. Her hair fell about his face like a fragrant silk veil. "Let's not be in such a hurry," she said shakily. "I want this to last."

He slid his hands up to either side of her face. In the moonlight she could see the shining, sapphire heat flaming in his eyes, and it made her feel weak with pleasure.

"I love you," he said softly, lifting his head to feather the tip of her ear with his lips.

April trembled as she felt the waiting heat in him. "I love you too. And I trust you. I finally realized that when you were standing up for me so boldly to Noble."

"Let me undress you."

She lay on her back, floating in a languid sea of love,

183

while he unbuttoned her dress and slipped it off, then, with hands that shook more noticeably as he progressed, pulled off her half-slip and panties and then her bra. He gazed down at her in the moonlight. "Let me look at you." His large hands touched her breasts reverently before moving over her stomach to the joining of her thighs. "Oh, God, you're beautiful," he groaned. With sudden haste his hands went to his belt buckle.

"No, let me." April sat up and pressed him down on the bed. Kneeling on the bed, she unbuckled his belt and pulled it free. Slowly she unzipped his trousers and began pushing them down his narrow hips.

He moved only enough to help her, reveling in this new April, the aggressor in their lovemaking. Her hands moved to the top button of his shirt; she undid the buttons, one by one, with agonizing slowness. By the time she had taken his shirt off, Vic was breathing so hard he sounded as though he'd been running for miles. Smiling softly, she put her hands on the waistband of his briefs and pushed them aside, revealing the hard strength of his manhood.

She touched him, and he groaned, catching his hands deeply in the tangle of her black hair and pulling her close to him.

"I'm yours forever, April," he whispered throatily. "Do whatever you want to do with me."

Deep inside her she felt a sudden releasing of her old doubts and inhibitions. Vic's love set her free to be bold. She kissed his chest, the crisp hairs grazing her lips as he held her to him. His male scent was incredibly arousing. She wanted to give him as much pleasure as he gave her, to bind him to her—and she acknowledged the selfish motive of the thought—as closely as she was bound to him.

She kissed each hard nipple, his stomach, then trailed feather-light kisses down the dark line that bisected his body. She heard him suck in air and was dazzled by her power to arouse and please. Like a wonder-struck explorer in a new land, her hands touched him in all the mysterious masculine places that so intrigued her. She felt the shuddering passion in him, held in check by the most tenuous of threads. When at last she came to the thrusting maleness of him, he cried out, "April!"

He pushed her back against the sheet. Her hair fanned out on the pillow, a dark frame for her lovely, pale face. "I'm crazy in love with you, crazy with wanting you!"

"Vic, my Vic . . ."

His hands slid beneath her to cup her hips and lift her up to meet him as he lost himself, with one swift thrust, in the intoxicating warmth and welcome of her body.

"There's no one like you in all the world," he gasped out. "Oh, God, April . . ."

Convulsively she wrapped her arms around him. "Oh!"

His mouth fused with hers as she arched her body to meet him. She surrendered to the consuming blaze of their passion and gave herself up to the rhythm of his lovemaking. Their mutual need and love were released in a tidal wave that swept over them until, for a few brief moments, it seemed that they shared one body and one dazzling range of sensations. April felt thoroughly loved and cherished and helpless at the same time that she felt powerful and free. She held him fiercely, shuddering as he cried her name with his own release.

For long moments, as the rippling waves subsided, they lay holding each other, incapable of moving or speaking.

Then Vic shifted his weight, pulled her back tightly into the curve of his body. He dropped a soft kiss on her damp forehead.

"Vic," she murmured, "will it always be like this?"

"Always," he promised, "even when we're old and gray and have a dozen children."

She chuckled drowsily. "Well, maybe two or three."

Placing his hand on her stomach, he pressed her even closer to him. "Thank you for that," he said, kissing her brow again.

"For what?"

"For saying that we can have children. It proves that you trust me completely."

She turned until she was facing him and wound her arms around his neck and kissed him. "Oh, I do, sweetheart!"

Vic smoothed the hair gently away from her face. "We don't have to live here. We'll buy a house. Whatever you want."

"The town house is fine—when we're in town. I've been thinking about hiring more help at the boutique so that I wouldn't have to go in every day. Then, if you could handle some of your business from the ranch, we could spend more time there. Oh, it'll be beautiful in the spring."

He lowered his mouth until it hovered a fraction of an inch from her parted lips. "You won't feel cut off, trapped?"

"I learned something this past week," she said decisively. "I could live in one room with you and Rusty and be free. Loving you makes me feel as though I could fly to the moon, or climb Mt. Everest—or do anything."

"And loving you," he murmured, "makes me so happy I can't see straight."

He kissed her, promising her that spring was only the beginning of innumerable seasons they would spend together.

LOOK FOR NEXT MONTH'S
CANDLELIGHT ECSTASY ROMANCES®

226 WINNER TAKE ALL, *Cathie Linz*
267 A WINNING COMBINATION, *Lori Copeland*
268 A COMPROMISING PASSION, *Nell Kincaid*
269 TAKE MY HAND, *Anna Hudson*
270 HIGH STAKES, *Eleanor Woods*
271 SERENA'S MAGIC, *Heather Graham*
272 DARE THE DEVIL, *Elaine Raco Chase*
273 SCATTERED ROSES, *Jo Calloway*

Candlelight
Ecstasy Romances™

- ☐ 242 **PRIVATE ACCOUNT**, Cathie Linz 17072-9-16
- ☐ 243 **THE BEST THINGS IN LIFE**, Linda Vail 10494-7-11
- ☐ 244 **SETTLING THE SCORE**, Norma Brader 17660-3-22
- ☐ 245 **TOO GOOD TO BE TRUE**, Alison Tyler 19006-1-13
- ☐ 246 **SECRETS FOR SHARING**, Carol Norris 17614-X-37
- ☐ 247 **WORKING IT OUT**, Julia Howard 19789-9-24
- ☐ 248 **STAR ATTRACTION**, Melanie Catley 18295-6-31
- ☐ 249 **FOR BETTER OR WORSE**, Linda Randall Wisdom 12558-8-10
- ☐ 250 **SUMMER WINE**, Alexis Hill Jordan 18353-7-14
- ☐ 251 **NO LOVE LOST**, Eleanor Woods 16430-3-23
- ☐ 252 **A MATTER OF JUDGMENT**, Emily Elliott 15529-0-35
- ☐ 253 **GOLDEN VOWS**, Karen Whittenburg 13093-X-10
- ☐ 254 **AN EXPERT'S ADVICE**, Joanne Bremer 12397-6-31
- ☐ 255 **A RISK WORTH TAKING**, Jan Stuart 17449-X-20
- ☐ 256 **GAME PLAN**, Sara Jennings 12791-2-25
- ☐ 257 **WITH EACH PASSING HOUR**, Emma Bennett 19741-4-21

$1.95 each

CANDLELIGHT
Ecstasy Supreme

All-new
Candlelight
Newsletter

**An exceptional,
free offer awaits readers
of Dell's incomparable Candlelight Ecstasy and Supreme Romances.**

Subscribe to our all-new CANDLELIGHT NEWSLETTER
and you will receive—at absolutely no cost to you—exciting, exclusive information about today's finest romance novels and nov-
elists. You'll be part of a select group to receive sneak previews of
upcoming Candlelight Romances, well in advance of publication.

You'll also go behind the scenes to "meet" our Ecstasy
and Supreme authors, learning firsthand where they get their
ideas and how they made it to the top. News of author appearances and events will be detailed, as well. And contributions from
the Candlelight editor will give you the inside scoop on how she
makes her decisions about what to publish—and how *you* can try
your hand at writing an Ecstasy or Supreme.

You'll find all this and more in Dell's CANDLELIGHT
NEWSLETTER. And best of all, *it costs you nothing.* That's right!
It's Dell's way of thanking our loyal Candlelight readers and of
adding another dimension to your reading enjoyment.

Just fill out the coupon below, return it to us, and look forward to receiving the first of many CANDLELIGHT NEWS-
LETTERS—overflowing with the kind of excitement that only
enhances our romances!

Return to: DELL PUBLISHING CO., INC.   B323D
         Candlelight Newsletter • Publicity Department
         245 East 47 Street • New York, N.Y. 10017

Name_____

Address_____

City_____

State_____Zip_____